True Things About Me

Also by Deborah Kay Davies

Grace, Tamar and Laszlo the Beautiful
Things You Think I Don't Know

True Things About Me

Deborah Kay Davies

CANONGATE

Edinburgh · London · New York · Melbourne

Published by Canongate Books in 2010

1

Copyright © Deborah Kay Davies, 2010

The moral right of the author has been asserted

First published in Great Britain in 2010 by Canongate Books Ltd,
14 High Street, Edinburgh EH1 1TE

www.meetatthegate.com

British Library Cataloguing-in-Publication Data
A catalogue record for this book is available on
request from the British Library

ISBN 978 1 84767 830 0

Typeset in Adobe Garamond by Palimpsest Book Production Ltd,
Falkirk, Stirlingshire

Printed and bound in Great Britain by CPI Mackays, Chatham ME5 8TD

For Norman,
with love

I go underground

I PRESSED THE buzzer for the next claimant. This old woman started telling me about her neighbour. As she spoke she kept tapping the glass barrier between us. That girl is on the game, she said, living off immoral earnings. It's disgusting. Someone ought to come round and investigate. I suggested she get in touch with the police. She pursed her lips and made a spitty sound. Probably half the police force are involved, she said, I wouldn't be surprised. Boys coming and going at all hours. And not only boys. Men too. Men old enough to be her granddad. She stood back and pointed with her thumb to her chest. I have seen men *my* age going in there.

I tried to take control of the interview, but she wasn't going to be put off. I could see a man with curly blond hair sitting behind and to the left of her. He had his arms crossed and his eyes closed. She leaned forward. And another thing, she said, there's always a lot of commotion; she's forever revving the engine of her fancy car outside my window, slamming doors, living like she doesn't have a care in the world. It shouldn't be allowed.

Every time the old woman banged the window she called me miss. I let her go on a bit while I looked over her shoulder at the other people waiting. I could see the guy was reading the paper now. Broad shoulders. His legs were long, stretched out in front of him, clad in faded, nicely tight jeans. I said to the woman, You leave this with me, we'll check it out, and scribbled down the address. She gave me a look. Thank you now, I said. I have to see the next claimant, and pressed my buzzer.

He sat down and leaned back in the chair. Name? I said, and wrote it down. I read his paperwork. He'd just come out of prison. Nothing serious, he said, and stretched. Just having a laugh with an articulated lorry and a lamp post. He settled back in the seat and grinned. I grinned back. I don't know why. It wasn't at all appropriate. Address? I said. He leaned near the barrier. Why d'you want to know? he said, his breath briefly etching an oval on the glass. I told him I was just doing my job. Nothing personal. Pity, he said. I leafed through his papers and picked up my pen. Married or single? I said. Single. Very, he said, and laid his hands palm down on the surface. Good hands, nice nails and what could have been a wedding ring.

I looked up from the forms. He winked. I told him he would have to wait about a week while someone processed his claim. No probs, he said. Is it your lunch-time soon? His shirt was open at the neck. His throat was kissable. No, I said, tidying up, I don't have time for lunch. Pity, he said again, and stood up. Everyone should have a break. You look as if you could do with a long one. I could feel myself starting to blush. I made a fuss of gathering up his paperwork. I couldn't bring myself to look up again. I pressed my buzzer and waited. Then he wasn't there.

Alison and I worked late. It was getting dark as we left the building, the air slightly chilly still. He was standing opposite the entrance. There's that man, I said to Alison. He was walking towards us. Which man? she said, peering around. Suddenly he was right in front of us. Hi, he said to me, ignoring her. Coming? Alison stood still and looked from him to me. Bye, I said and shrugged my shoulders. Alison held onto my arm. What about the film? she said quietly. He took hold of my hand and pulled me gently. I just went. Alison called out, Are you sure you're all right? I tried to answer but we were walking too fast, we were too far away, already going underground.

I don't value my possessions

HE TOOK ME down the steps into the car park, and led me to a dark area. I could smell damp concrete, oil, exhaust fumes. He backed me up against a pillar. Take your underwear off, he said, and grinned, showing his teeth. Stand on me. I mean, stand on my shoes. You mustn't get your feet dirty. He supported me while I struggled out of my tights and knickers. My mind had stretched and blanked, like a washed sheet on a clothes line. He had one arm round my waist. He put his hand up between my legs and pressed his fingers inside. I love the way that feels, he said. Then he unzipped his trousers and pushed his penis into my hand. It tapped heavily against my palm.

I'm so ready, he said. Are you? Yes, I said, and opened my legs for him. Say fuck me, he said, so I did. He grunted as he pushed himself in. I locked my arms round his neck. He sucked my bottom lip. I licked his teeth with my tongue. I felt his shoelaces under the arches of my feet. As he came I whacked the back of my head hard against the pillar. Afterwards I heard car doors slamming, and my legs gave way.

Short and sweet, he said, as he sorted my clothes out. He picked me up and carried me to the taxi rank. We didn't speak. He helped me into a cab and paid the driver. You might want these some time, he said, and threw the screwed-up knot of tights and knickers inside. See you around. All right, mate, he said to the taxi driver and banged the roof of the car. I sat on the seat with my underwear in my hands. I investigated the bruise on my head with my fingers; it felt tacky. Semen seeped out of me and pooled onto my skirt. When I got home I saw that the back of my new leather coat was scratched and scored. I bundled it up and chucked it in the bottom of my cupboard. I'd only had it for a week.

I get reflective

THAT NIGHT I began to be afraid; I couldn't remember things like how to do my job. I switched on the bedside lamp and made notes. I tried to jot down some tasks I needed to do in the morning, but in the end I just wrote: turn on computer; make coffee; file answered paperwork in alphabetical order. Then I wrote a new list and put the first, draft list in alphabetical order. It seemed like a complicated task. The period of time after I'd left work was incomprehensible. I knew I should think about it. The easiest way would be in terms of colour. Mid-blue was coming out of work with Alison. Suddenly yellow. Then apricot. Down into red, streaked with something else. At the bottom a sediment of khaki.

The next morning I decided to ring Alison and ask her to tell our boss I was sick. I avoided the big mirror on the wardrobe in my bedroom, and walked through the quiet house down the stairs to the kitchen. Everything was in place. I could barely lift the phone to my ear. The lead was kinked into snarled-up shapes. Alison answered eventually. Hang on, she said, before I'd spoken a word. Then I heard her shouting something about lunch boxes, and the sounds of running up and down stairs. Then a door slammed.

Right, she said, they've gone. How are you this morning? I, before you ask, have never been fabber. I just live for school-day mornings. Oh, the joy of tuna and mayo sarnies. The giddy search for bloody swimming cossies. Suddenly I couldn't remember what I'd rung for. Go on, I said. Alison's voice was like a cool hand on my forehead. Let me see, she said. You want me to tell old fridge-baps you're sick. Is that it? If you would, I said. My voice was unfamiliar. All in a day's work, she said. Are you all right? I've been so worried about you. 'Course, I said. Why shouldn't I be? Duh, ooh, I can't think why, she said with what I thought was unnecessary sarcasm. Well, I'll be speaking to you in depth very soon, young lady. Can't wait, I said.

I made myself coffee. Sunlight pulsed in the kitchen, bouncing off the kettle and the utensils in the rack. I had some chocolate left, so I carried that and the coffee upstairs. Finally I stood in front of the mirror and let my robe fall off my shoulders. Would you look at yourself, I said to my reflection in a take-the-piss Irish accent. My face was the same, but not the same. It looked slyly back at me, the eyes smaller, paler maybe. I felt afraid again. I reached up to touch the back of my head. The hair felt like a small, painful nest. I looked at myself properly. You're filthy, I said. How could you do those things? But I couldn't keep the accent up. My smiling mouth in the mirror shocked me.

In the bathroom I ran a bath. It hurt to pee. I didn't recognise the smell of myself. Each time I thought about the car park, something winced in the pit of my stomach and a fluttering sensation rose up from around my heart and drifted out through my scalp. I felt appalled. In the bath the water swam over me. I sank under and worked the dried blood out of my hair. As I did, the fluttering sensation changed. Now it felt like something was shrivelling inside. I remembered banging my head. Tears slid into my ears. I scrabbled out of the bath and dried myself.

The house was profoundly silent, every room empty. It felt like an out-of-season holiday home. I couldn't spend time there, so I put on some clothes, slammed the front door and got in my car. At the traffic lights I avoided my reflection in the rear-view mirror while I sent a text to Alison: Will be entering the building ASAP. Thank god 4 flexitime. Luv u.

I worked like a maniac all day and skipped lunch. I ignored Alison's concerned glances, organised some leave and left my desk tidy. Lastly I made a note of his address and phone number, just in case.

I talk to the animals

I DECIDED TO visit my grandmother. Magazines were always saying that if you were feeling down the best plan was to do something for someone else. I couldn't find her in the ward. All the old ladies looked the same to me. My gran had been the busty, blue rinse, costume jewellery sort of gran. She used to make me little crisp golden tarts with strawberry jam in the centre. Each one was decorated with a pastry letter from my name. The molten jam was lethal. We sewed clothes for my doll, Valerie. Gran said we should concentrate on evening wear for Valerie. Val's that type of girl, she said, winking. We winked at each other a lot. We spent rainy days colouring in together. Never you mind, she said, when I went outside the lines. Nobody's perfect, my darling. Least of all your granny.

I walked round the ward and looked at each old lady. They all seemed like half-inflated balloons. Finally I found her and sat down on the shiny armchair beside her bed. I picked up her hand. I didn't recognise the rings she was wearing. Gran?

I said. She turned her head to look at me. We stared at each other. Are you my gran? I asked. The nurse came in. Yours is over there, she said, picking up a chart that was hooked over the end of the bed. She had to help me extricate my hand. The old lady had a strong grip. As we struggled with her she made a sort of keening sound.

I found myself in the toilet. For God's sake, I said in the cubicle. For goddy God's sake. I sat on the loo with the lid down and started to laugh. My laugh had a shake in it. In the echoing toilet it sounded eerie. That made me laugh even more. Then I cried. Someone used the loo next to me so I cried silently. There was a sound of rustling, and I stopped to listen. Then a genteel fart. Excuse me, a voice said, as the flush went. I giggled feebly until my sobbing stopped, and went out to wash my hands and repair my face. There was a handwritten sign over the basin: Beware. Dangerously hot water. The ink had run so it was like some spooky warning from a mirror in a horror film. I used the cold tap. Right, I said. Now for my gran.

I kissed her forehead. She used to smell of Coty face powder and polo mints. She patted my cheek. How are you, my little love? she said. Her eyes were like tiny chocolatey berries. I told her all about the blond man. I described him in detail. She gazed at me and faintly smiled. When I told her about the car park and the taxi, her eyebrows moved. I thought she might have winked. Gran, I said, I feel really bad. But nobody's perfect, are they? Right? She squeezed my fists with her warm hands. I felt calmer.

I told her it seemed like some sort of turning point. What do you think? I asked. What should I do now? Not see him again? Her nightdress was trimmed around the neckline with rosebuds, and a plastic slide held her hair away from her face. I waited. She opened her lips and began to make the sounds of a chicken, quietly at first. I dropped her hands. Then she threw her head back and started crowing like a cockerel. She had little claws that plucked the bedclothes. I couldn't move. The nurse appeared and touched my shoulder. You should go now, she said, and gave me a shake. It's time for her meds.

I am abandoned by my mother

AFTER MY VISIT to the nursing home I couldn't sleep. Poor old Gran, she would have hated to be herself now. I remembered the sound of her high heels clacking around her kitchen. She wouldn't have been seen dead wearing slippers, let alone a hair clip. All night my eyelids were stretched round my bulging eyeballs. In the morning I felt as if I'd aged five years in the dark, so I decided to go to the surgery.

My usual doctor was away. I saw a locum instead, a gorgeous-looking Asian woman. It was difficult to tell how old she was. I imagined she must be somewhere between twelve and forty-five. Not twelve, of course, that was ridiculous. But still, she might have been. She didn't take her eyes off her computer screen. Yes? she said. Problems? No, I said. I'm really, really, really great. How are you? She finally looked at me. What can I do to help? she asked flatly. I told her I needed something to make me sleep. She frowned. Have you had sleeping pills before? she asked, and returned to the computer. Finally she gave me a prescription.

I busied myself around the house for the rest of the day. I had an old film on DVD I'd been meaning to see, so in the afternoon I sat down to watch it. Things start off with this very beautiful woman, who seems normal; innocent and good. But soon you realise she's crazy. Her husband writes plays and she stalked him into agreeing to marry her by pretending to be mad about the theatre. It was one of those films where the viewer knows things long before the people in the film do. Eventually she drowns her trusting new husband's sweet, crippled brother and destroys her own unborn child, because she's jealous of any attention her beloved gives to anyone else. Then, after plotting to incriminate him in her death, she poisons herself. All because he's found out what she's done, and is going to leave her. As she dies of poisoning, lying there against the pillows like a dark angel, she tells him, *I'll never let you go, never, never*. God, she was evil. But you had to sympathise with her somehow; she definitely knew what she wanted. Although I couldn't understand what she saw in him; he was a complete drip, and he had improbably groomed eyebrows.

I turned the TV off and began to think about the car park again. I saw myself slipping out of my shoes. Taking off my underwear. He had helped me. I remembered the cold air moving up inside my skirt, the feel of his muscular back and the way he sort of stooped over to grab my mouth with his.

I thought about holding him in my hand. I took some of the tablets and went to bed. I couldn't stop going over it all. When I thought about how he'd grunted as he pushed his penis inside me I felt a buzzing sensation between my legs, accompanied by a delicious little flip.

In bed I kept trying to find cool places on my pillows. Then I fell asleep. I dreamed I was out with my mother. I was a child; she loomed over me as we walked. She was singing a hymn to herself in time with the rhythm of our steps. We passed a dark alley, its entrance partially obscured by trails of ivy blowing in a non-existent wind. My mother pushed me into the alley. I could still hear her singing. There was a line of rubbish bins along the wall. In slow motion a huge black bear with blood on its teeth reared up out of one of the bins. The bin lid stayed on its head like a stiff flat cap. It lunged at me and scooped out my stomach with its curved claws.

I heard my spine snap. Splat went all my organs on the floor. My middle was crimson and empty. I felt the cold air playing on the raw, hot flesh. I screamed for my mother, but she didn't answer. She just went on singing and swinging her handbag out in the sunlit street. I woke up half out of bed, breathless and covered in a film of perspiration. I stood under the shower and then wrapped myself in an old towelling robe. Downstairs I poured some apple juice and sat at the kitchen table until it got light.

I serve unusual nibbles

I BEGAN TO hover near the cupboard where I'd slung my damaged leather jacket. You've got to deal with stuff like this, you silly girl, I said out loud. I had been reading a magazine article called 'Moving On, Moving Up'. I knew it was all crap, but somehow I couldn't stop thinking about my jacket. I lay on the bed and talked to myself. What was the matter with me, anyway? There were lots of perfectly nice, normal girls who did stuff in underground car parks all the time. Nobody judged them. They had a giggle about it with their mates around the photocopier for God's sake.

But I thought about my jacket. I remembered how long it had taken to save the money. The soft, butterscotch-coloured skin. How it felt light and cool, though it protected me perfectly from the cold wind. Its intoxicating smell. I thought about the knubby wooden buttons with their metal shanks. Everything's ruined now, I said.

When I opened the cupboard door, the wholesome, throaty

smell of leather poured out. I stepped back and breathed in deeply. The smell was peaceful. It reminded me of the school satchel my cousin Daniel had handed down to me. There were strange bits of writing on the strap; ragged, scratched-in symbols. They were the things Daniel had done. So it was new to me, but not new; it had been to school before. The leather was soft and shiny in the places Daniel had worn it. I remembered my school beret being snatched off my head as I'd walked up the drive for the first time. But no one had wanted the old satchel that I loved. That little girl wouldn't have gone down into an underground car park when she grew up. She was not the sort of girl who would spoil a valuable coat for nothing.

I looked at the sleeping tablets on the bedside table. I'd emptied them out of their plastic strips and put them in a little bowl. It was funny how they looked like the courtesy mints you get offered in some restaurants. I picked up the bowl and offered it to my reflection. Do have some, won't you? I said in the voice of Judith Chalmers, my gran's favourite travel presenter. Take a handful, feel free! I promised myself that after I'd looked at my poor coat properly I'd take some and sleep for days. I walked round the room, and read my magazine for a bit. I'd bought it because of the caption on the front cover, announcing an article about a woman who'd been knocked out by a frozen oven chip.

There were other discarded things in the bottom of the cupboard, so I rummaged until I felt the jacket. The lining was slippery and chill to the touch. It wasn't as heavy as I'd thought. I spent some time arranging it on the crumpled duvet. It seemed too small for me to wear. More like a little girl's coat. Or the flying jacket of a tiny, old-fashioned, aero-stunt pilot. I felt it with my hands, like a blind girl might do, and thought how I would never wear it again. I flipped it over, and pushed my fingers inside the cuts. I heard someone sobbing. The lacerations looked as if they'd been inflicted by an animal.

I advise on sartorial issues

ALISON ASKED HOW long my leave was going to last. And why I'd suddenly taken it. I felt too tired to say anything. She held up a sheeny black dress and said, What d'you think? Is it me? Try it on, I said. Who can tell when it's on the hanger? I followed her into the communal changing room. Is this leave thing about last week? You might as well know I've forgiven you for your desertion, she said. Though I don't approve, of course. I will say just one thing at this juncture: I can't understand what came over you.

Juncture? I said. Juncture? What sort of poncey word is that? Juncture is not a word I ever thought I'd hear fall from your ruby lips. Whatever, she said, posing in the mirror. Don't think I don't know what you're doing with this juncture business. It won't work. Her reflection gave me a mean look. Stick to the point, she said, turning to face me. I was silent, so she sighed, narrowing her eyes, and started to tell me about the party she and Tom were going to. She said it was Tom's head

23

office do. A chance to meet his boss, and she really needed to make a statement. She reached down inside the front of the dress to reposition her breasts. Hoick those puppies up, I said. Her reflection looked at me. Have you been listening to me? she asked. Only I have the feeling I'm boring you.

I slid down the wall and sat on the changing-room floor. Obviously chairs were obsolete. Alison was adjusting the dress round her hips. I hope you are taking note that I'm using superhuman restraint in not insisting on a detailed account of your impromptu evening with Mr Blond, she said. What's Tom wearing to this? I said. Will he have his tits out as well? Alison gave me a look. I could see she was counting up to ten. I'm sorry, I said. Actually I gave Mr Blond the elbow not long after you went. I could tell he was bad news. Oh God, I'm so relieved, she said. So you're not seeing him again? I thought of how he'd banged the taxicab roof and walked away. Definitely not, I said. I'm not that desperate. Her reflection gave me a kind look.

She did a twirl in the black dress. I'm not sure about this bias cut thing, she said. Where do you stand on bias? Darling, I said, nowadays, if it's not bias I refuse to give it the time of day. Even my bra is bias cut. And the gusset of your knickers? she asked. Double bias with extra bias at the back and sides, I said. You really are in a weird mood, she said, and squinted at her behind in the mirror, then at me with a questioning look. Before you ask, I said, your bum looks positively microscopic. Actually, where is your bum? I've got a

vibe you don't like this ensemble, she said, but one happens
to think one looks hot, so one's going to have to buy it at
this juncture. Sod the expense, I said, one should always go
for it.

I make people materialise

SUDDENLY I ACTUALLY wanted to see my parents. When I got there things were just the same. I sat down and had a cup of tea with my mother. I asked her how she was. The clock in the hall ticked familiarly, its wheeze still detectable. Musn't grumble, she said. Though you'd love to, my dad's voice added from the hallway. Any news on the boyfriend front? she asked, not looking at me. I may have, I said. Immediately she was riveted. Well, she said, I just hope he's a nice boy. You've always been so trusting. She patted my knee. But that's a good fault, of course, she said. My father's mild voice drifted in from the kitchen this time: There's no such thing as a good fault, as you well know. Faults are bad. That's the way they are. My mother smiled at me. Oh well, you understand what I mean, don't you, darling?

She wanted to know about my boyfriend. I told her he was five years older than me. Dark, straight hair. Actually, I said, he has these improbably well-groomed eyebrows. She thought for a while. But that's good, she said, the groomed aspect, I mean. So many young men are too casual about grooming. He's not gay though, is he? I'm not sure, I said. Only time will tell. I told her he was a writer. I didn't know I was going to say that, but it sounded good as soon as I did. It's quite sad really, I added. He has this really sweet younger brother he's devoted to, but the poor boy is disabled.

I began to see my boyfriend clearly. He had nice hands. He was absolutely mad about me. I'm meeting him tonight, I said. Well, I'm happy for you, she said. It's about time. No offence, darling. You know I love you. Miraculously, as I looked at him, my boyfriend's hair turned blond and started to tighten into curls.

I said I'd stay for lunch. In the kitchen my mother held my chin in her hand and scrutinised me. You look a little peaky, she said. Are you eating properly? I know you snack, but do you sit down and actually eat a meal? I told her I was feeling under the weather. Is that why you're off work? she asked. God, Mum, I said, do you pay someone to snoop on me? I am an adult, you know. She ignored me and went on to say how glad she was I had a friend like lovely Alison. She's so sensible, she said, turning her back on me so I could tie her apron. Anyway, you're a very lucky girl, you know. So is Alison, I said, to have lovely me. She gave me a busy hug. Well, of course, dear, she said. That goes without saying. Now I have to get on. Things won't cook themselves.

My dad took me out into the garden. He wanted to show

me the bronze fennel. I love it, I said. The delicate fronds were woven into a glinting series of loose nets. At the heart of each net was what looked like a big fuzzy caterpillar. We both stooped down to check them out. They were actually the still-sheathed buds, almost ready to shake themselves into life. We sat on a garden bench and I ran my fingers through the swaying plant. I told my dad it felt like ropy, damp hair. Almost like a mermaid's. He had a feel. You're right, it does, he said. I could always tell my father things like that, when we were on our own. I rested my head on his shoulder, and held his rough, gardener's hand. I was about to say something when Mum shouted for his help. Got to go. Duty calls, he said, saluting, and left me.

The fennel smelled like aniseed. It reminded me of some ointment Gran used to put on my cuts and bruises. I sat alone in the shade, the fern swaying beside me, and watched a cloud of tiny black butterflies discover the scarlet runner-bean flowers. Someone was using an old-fashioned lawnmower, the sound like some giant clock's mechanism ratcheting the hundreds of seconds away. Warm, dry moss covered the arms of the bench like upholstery. I sank into a garden trance, and watched the bed of dahlias glow, their spiny heads radiating red sunlight. Behind them, I could see the lilac flounces of some other plant billow up. A spider trickled over the back of my hand.

I heard my mother tinkling cutlery in the house. The roast lamb smelled delicious. I stood up just as she called out, asking me to pick a bunch of mint. As I chose the bright, hairy stalks I found I was crying happily into them. The perfume of the mint wafted around me and purified everything. I strolled around the garden, touching things: the sweet pea canes, the rough, juicy rhubarb leaves, the warm wood of my dad's shed. I found I could move from one thing to another without the slightest effort, almost by just thinking about where I felt like going. I never wanted to leave.

After lunch I stayed on. We sat in the afternoon garden and let it soak into us. We were all quiet. Once I heard the ice cream van's ribbon of music trailing through the streets, but it seemed very far away. My dad asked me if I would like to stay the night. I thought about my little bedroom, kept just as I'd left it, and said yes. What about your date? my mum asked. I told her I'd put him off. He won't mind, I said. You want to hold onto him, she said. He sounds very understanding.

My father brought me some cushions, and lying on the bench in the semi-shade I fell asleep watching fat blobs of sunlight slipping back and forth over my body. I didn't dream at all. When I woke up we had gin and tonics. My favourite sound, my mother said, and jostled her ice cubes. Every now and then my father would get up and pull some microscopic weed. There was a faint smell of spring onions rising from a neat little bed he'd planted next to his roses. You've got to root the little blighters out, he said.

I misuse bread

WHEN I GOT home I began to feel like a visitor, or a prospective buyer. I wandered through the rooms of my house but I couldn't see its potential. Time started to do that thing. It's like you're from some other dimension where each minute is an hour and a half, say, but an hour is actually a day long. You're trying to function in your new body, with your new watch on your strange, pink arm, but you just don't fool anyone. The safest approach when this happens is to sit in one place and wait for something to occur.

Eventually I heard the phone ringing. Alison wanted to come and see me. We sat in the kitchen. She looked in the fridge and made a tutting sound. Well, at least you've got some milk, she said. She told me she couldn't be long. That she just wanted to touch base, see me, sort of thing. You can touch my base any time, love, I said, and we both cackled. I told her I would be back to work on Monday, which I was quite surprised about myself. I didn't know I was going to do that.

Alison told me her kids were at their karate class, and she had to pick them up soon. Aren't they a bit young for martial arts? I asked. I knew they were only four and six. Also there was a baby of about a year old. She struck what looked like a karate pose and said, Ah! Never too young, my doubting and defenceless friend. Surely not the baby, though, I asked. 'Course not, she said. Check me out. She held up her thumbs and wiggled them around. I could disable an attacker using just these, she said seriously. Really? I said. No, she answered, but that sort of skill would be invaluable in the rush for the only empty checkout.

She wanted to know if I could babysit the two older ones on Saturday morning for a few hours. She had to take her mum to an appointment at the eye clinic and couldn't cope with all the kids as well. On a Saturday? I asked. Private, she said. Cataracts. You know my mum. Money no object. Except when I try and touch her for a tenner. Are you sure you want me to? I said. I mean, I like your kids, but do you think I should look after them? She told me not to be wet, that they were becoming more like human beings all the time. I would be fine.

The complication is I have to go to the dentist for a filling, I said. Won't that scare them? She said they loved the dentist. They wouldn't mind at all. Especially if they could watch; they liked watching people having dental treatment. I wasn't sure that was healthy. If that's true, I said, then they are small but perfectly formed fiends. Yep, she said, you are not far wrong, oh wise one. Anyway, she didn't have anyone else to ask. Tom was refereeing a match or something. Pray for me, she said. I've got to take the baby with us. And you and I still haven't had our significant chat about you know what. I told her that, actually, we didn't need to. It wasn't an issue. I'll be the judge of that, kiddo, she said.

On Saturday I picked the children up. They sat in the back of the car with their little rucksacks full of kids' stuff, exuding vital energy, like meerkats. Their shining hair seemed to swing of its own volition. I couldn't detect any blinking of their eyes. Before we drove off I asked them if they remembered me. Nope, they said firmly. That's probably a good thing, I said. Last time I checked you were Harriet and Patrick. I'm the oldest, Patrick said, leaning towards me. She's only four. Well, you two, I said, I am old beyond your wildest dreams of oldness, and my name is Mrs Blobbypants. Harriet took her thumb out of her mouth for a moment. Mrs Bloppypants the Third, she said. I told her she was a bright kid. I'm even brighter, said Patrick. That's because I'm older than her.

There seemed to be a lot of movement in the car. I asked them to keep still. We wasn't moving, actually, Patrick said, was we, Harriet? Well, anyway, I said, and asked them what they wanted to do. Watch TV, they said in unison. Isn't that the standard kids' answer? I asked them. They didn't say anything. TV it is then, I said brightly. We like TV best of all, they said, nodding at each other and me intently. Even

33

more than karate? I asked. Karate's cool, said Patrick, but TV's cooler, isn't it, Harriet? Harriet smiled round her thumb, and nodded gently as if she were conserving energy for later. I told them I had some things to do first. Like the dentist. Cool, Patrick said. The dentist is excellent, we love the dentist. Can we watch?

When we got there I bought them comics and sweets in the newsagent's next door. My stomach was behaving the way it always did whenever I entered the waiting room. When I was little my father had to have time off work to take me; my mother had given up on the whole thing. I remember holding onto the treatment room door handle and screaming with complete abandon. It seemed to me that all the grown-ups had changed and become cruel people. My mother and father, the smiling receptionist, the kind-looking dentist – they had all betrayed me. They were prepared to offer me up to anything that might happen. There was this feeling of utter aloneness.

I explained to the nurse that the children wanted to come in to watch. She looked down at them unsmilingly. Do you now? she asked them. I don't s'pose that will be a problem. She directed them to a single chair, and told them they'd have to be quiet. They sat facing the huge black affair I had to sit in. I remembered what Alison had said when she dropped the kids off about creating only positive dental vibes. The dentist came towards me with the needle held behind his back. I can see it, shouted Harriet. My heart plunged like a body dropping off the top of a high-rise block of flats. The children leaned forward as I was injected in the softest, most private parts of my mouth. Then the dentist turned to chat to them. I limply allowed the chair to support all my weight.

When the drill started shrilling Harriet got down from the chair and came a little nearer. I gave them both a thumbs-up sign. My hand was shaking. Afterwards, in the car, they sucked with intense concentration on the sweets I'd bought them, fingering the stickers they'd picked up at the dentist. You should give those to me, I told them over my shoulder. I was the flipping brave one. I wasn't joking either. We drove to town. They asked when they could watch TV. Very soon, believe me, I said. They started to fiddle with each other. She's just pinched me; he's pulled my hair. That sort of thing. My jaw was fizzing and beginning to ache. I felt as if my knee joints were turning molten. We went into a bread shop.

I counted four people in front of me. Each one had an enormous bread order. I wondered what that was about; so much stupid bread. I felt light-headed, as if the top section of my skull was exposed to the air. I picked up a long baguette from a deep wicker basket. It was strangely quiet in the shop, except for the sounds of the children slapping each other and scuffling. They both bumped into me sharply several times. It was weird, but it felt as if they were somehow disturbing my newly-filled tooth, jabbing it even. Suddenly I swung round and whacked both of them on the tops of their heads with the baguette. Everyone in the shop turned to look at me. I stood holding the broken stick of bread. The woman behind the counter nodded at it. I hope you intend to pay for that, she said. I had to wait my turn. No one else spoke. When we got outside Patrick put his arm round Harriet and said, loudly and calmly, We hate you. When we get home I'm going to tell my mum you hit us with bread.

I always deliver

I'D PUT HIS address in a kitchen drawer. It was the one I kept my sharp knives in. I had opened it a few times, to get knives out. There it was, every time. So I sat in the kitchen and allowed the steam from my coffee to lap my face. My tooth was quietly humming. I took some painkillers, but I didn't mind the pain. When I thought about the dentist I felt a little spasm of pleasure that I'd managed to get through it. As soon as I thought about the filling I remembered the children and the bakery. I wondered why Alison hadn't rung me.

It had rained with surprising intensity since early morning. The kitchen window was open and, rhythmically, the garden's rainy breath gushed into the room. The blind worried itself in the breeze, but I couldn't be bothered to sort it out. I heard a police car's wailing scream. Then more. All rushing towards the motorway. I imagined the accident they were attending. I played it out in my head. I saw the car, crushed like a cartoon car in a cartoon wreck. There were little petals of fire escaping from the distorted bonnet. I watched pools of blood creeping out from under the driver's door.

I remembered the time I had driven past an accident and seen the dead driver. His arm, in a short-sleeved shirt, was flung out from under a makeshift covering. I had burst into passionate tears as I drove slowly past, thinking how he must have been on his way to work on an ordinary day. How his wife and children didn't even know yet that he was dead. How I, a stranger, did know. It hadn't felt at all right to have this knowledge before them. I'd cried all day at work, and gone home early, then lain on my bed in the darkened bedroom and thought about the dead man. He'd been wearing a business-like watch on his flung-out, muscular arm. His fingers had been furled in towards his palm, gently, as if he were holding something fragile, something he didn't want to crush. I kept thinking about how his fingers had curled inwards for the last time. And that whatever he'd wanted to protect didn't matter any more. It was probably nothing, just fresh, free air. No use to him now.

My coffee was cool, so I must have been sitting there for a while; these days I could almost measure time in cooling cups of coffee. It was a new skill, but quite handy. I threw the coffee away and made another. I opened the knife drawer and took out the little folded slip of paper. I smoothed it flat on the table and let it lie by the side of my fresh cup. He lived in an unfamiliar area of town. Vaguely I knew where it was. I didn't want my coffee any more so I left it on the table and put the piece of paper in my bag.

I showered and dressed. I went out and bought flowers and candles, red wine and cheese. The flowers were squeaky-stemmed tulips, flame coloured, with frilly green edges. When I got home I cleaned the house and arranged the tulips in a pale pink vase. I put the cheese on a plate and opened the wine. I laid out the flowers and everything else on the coffee table. I changed into my nightdress. It was getting dark, still raining. I lit candles in the lounge.

I put the film in the DVD player and watched it again. This time I loathed the beautiful woman. She was so false. I don't know how I could have been taken in for so long the first time. The writer guy was lovely, though. God, did she make him suffer. It took him so long to comprehend how bad she really was. All through the film his eyebrows hardly moved, but I could tell when he was upset. As I watched I drank the wine and ate the cheese. It felt like a ritual. As he was taken off to prison, unjustly accused of her murder, I raised my glass to him. Good luck, my darling, I said. I must have fallen asleep on the settee for a while, because when I awoke the candles had burned down in the cold room. There was a smell of smoke coming from the wicks. It was one o'clock in the morning. I threw some clothes on, took my bag and drove to his address.

I found the house easily. It was almost spooky. I seemed to know exactly where it was. I parked the car opposite and turned off the engine. I was still drunk, but I felt in control. Some windows in the street were alight. There was a downstairs light on in his house. I sat and looked at the yellow rectangle it cast. Then I got out of the car and walked across the road, through a broken gate and up the path. The garden was overgrown. The front door had scratches on it. A small fanlight window above it was smashed. I knocked on the door. A dog barked inside and someone shouted. I felt calm.

There was a long wait, but I didn't knock again. A pale woman with a sunken chest appeared. I asked for him by name. She said she'd never heard of him. I got my notebook from my bag and ripped out a page. She stood holding a cigarette. She didn't seem in the least bit interested in me. Could you give him this? I said. It's important. I handed her the note I'd written. The dog padded towards me and licked my leg. She took the piece of paper without looking at it, and said she couldn't promise anything. As I walked back to my car she leaned against the doorpost and watched. I heard her coughing. As I drove off she was still leaning there with the dog beside her. I started to tremble. I stopped the car when I got out of sight, and opened the door just in time to be sick onto the road. Then I drove home.

I keep in touch

ALISON AND I had lunch in a café near the office. Why can't I just have a good old British sandwich? she asked. Why must it be ciabatta and wraps and stuff like that? Who's Panini anyway? He sounds like a composer. I blame all this foreign travel. Everyone should be made to go to Skegness and Bognor. Then we'd all be eating limp ham sarnies and drinking tea in buckets. I have nothing against a wrap occasionally, I said. And it's a well-known factoid that the poor unfortunate souls who end up in Skegness need more than a wrap to survive. They need SAS-type clothing. Alison looked around. I'm not sure about this place, she said; it's suspiciously empty for a lunchtime.

I was happy for Alison to go off on a food rant. It postponed talking about the bread-hitting incident, so I made a decided effort to keep it going. Anyway, I said, nobody in living memory has been to Bognor. Isn't Bognor a tropical free-love island now? Towed out to the Maldives? I thought

I read about it in *Hello!* Alison was studying the menu. When the waitress came I recognised her, she was a girl I'd known slightly in school. Hi, she said. Long time no see. You could say that, I said. Like aeons and aeons. True, she said, holding up her little pad and pen. I s'pose I'll have one of these tortilla things, Alison said, and a cup of tea. I asked the waitress if she did ham sandwiches. We do, she said. Can you make mine a limp one? I asked. You always were a funny person, she said. When our food came Alison gazed longingly at my plate. I told her she could have mine if she would forgive me about hitting her kids with bread.

Listen, my lovely young friend, she said. I don't blame you. I once smacked their legs with an Easter egg. They can wind one up, believe me, I know. I told her I was feeling a bit tense at the time, what with my filling. If anything, it's my fault, she said. I know how you feel about the dentist. But are you all right, you know, generally? I replied that I was great. That I had just needed some time off. I told her she was very sweet to be so understanding. Well, it's not as if you repeatedly bashed their heads in with a mallet, is it? she said. But here's a thought for today. Are we both a bit nuts, chastising children with food items? All the same, I apologise, I said. It was horrible of me. I accept your apology, she said, and ate my sandwich.

On the way home from work I drove past his house. There were some small children messing about in the grotty front garden. The dog that had licked my leg was leaping about.

One of the kids had a flag on a short pole, and he was waving it enthusiastically inches from the heads of the others. That's all I could see as I drove along the road. When I got home I looked at the piece of paper with his address on it. There was also a telephone number. I hadn't registered it, all the times I had looked, which was odd. I sat on the sofa with the phone and the note. I knew I would call the number eventually. I was almost in no hurry to do it. The longer I sat the slower my heart beat. I could hear its drumming tailing off in my ears. I began to feel that this time, on my own, on the sofa, was a precious time. I felt sure that he would soon be with me. He must have got my note by now. What was more normal than to follow up a letter with a friendly phone call?

I entertain at home

I WAS LOOKING for the key in my bag when he appeared behind me. In the small porch he looked enormous. I invited him in. I got all your little messages, he said, sounding amused. So here I am. What do you want? His voice was surprisingly soft, confidential even. He had a way of turning sideways when he spoke, as if he might bolt away at any moment. It made me want to hold onto him, but I didn't. I liked the way he filled the hallway.

Coffee? I asked, walking ahead of him, trying to keep my voice normal. He said he wanted something stronger. I only had Martini and gin. Don't bother, he said. What have you got to eat? He roamed around downstairs. For such a large person he was a quiet walker. I stood in the kitchen and looked in the fridge. Cottage cheese, I called out. Salad, some eggs. I could go out and get something. OK, he said. Where's the remote?

I left him draped on the sofa watching TV, and went to

the supermarket in my car. I tried to drive carefully. All the shoppers were drifting around the store in slow motion. I wanted to smash them with my basket. I bought some chocolate for myself, Jack Daniels, thick-cut bacon, crusty bread and spicy sausages. Somehow I knew he wasn't vegetarian. I gobbled half the chocolate down as I drove home. I was sure he would be gone when I got back, but there he was, stretched out on the sofa. Someone called Alison rang, he said, still looking at the TV screen. I told her you'd left the country.

After he'd eaten he said, Come on, baby, and held out his arms. He kissed me all over my face; succulent, bacony kisses. He told me to bring the chocolate. In my bedroom he laid me on my bed and closed the curtains. My room felt strange. He expertly took off my clothes. Now you do me, he said. I stripped off his socks. His feet were beautiful. The nails square and smooth. I struggled with his jeans. He lifted his hips up so I could pull them down. His erection sprang out at me. Don't bother with my shirt, he said. Now I want you to sit on this. I straddled him and lowered myself down slowly. He pushed a square of chocolate into my mouth. It turned to liquid immediately. I seemed to feel him near my heart. There was a buried ache. Baby, he said, you're lovely, aren't you? I don't know how to do this, I said. I thought I would cry.

He lifted me off. I lay on my front and he caressed my back and buttocks. Can't wait any longer, he said, and flipped me over and pushed a pillow under my hips. I held onto him tightly with my arms, and crossed my legs behind his back.

I pressed my nose into his fine, curly hair. My tongue tasted sweet and creamy to me. Later when I woke he'd gone. There was a note on the kitchen table. 'Got to run. Back later probably,' it said.

I am not always available

IT WAS DIFFICULT to concentrate in the office. I kept wanting to look at myself in the mirror. My boss asked if I was all right. I told her I'd never felt better, which was true in a way. It was a hectic feeling, and I was incapable of sitting still. Interviewing claimants was challenging. I kept thinking of how I first saw him, lounging on a screwed-down chair in the waiting room. In the loo I stared at myself. The strip lighting gave my skin a translucent look. My lips seemed too dark to be mine. I had circles that were palest grey beneath my eyes. I looked like a woman with secrets.

Alison followed me in. Hail, silent and slightly nutty one, she said and smiled at me. Hang on while I have a wee. I was happy to go on examining my reflection. I rang you, she said from inside the cubicle. Some bloke answered the phone. I met my reflection's eyes. Who was it? she asked as she came out to wash her hands. No one important, I said. We combed our hair. She looked brown and rosy in the mirror. I was fascinated by the contrast between us.

OK, be secretive, she said, but I have a nasty idea who it might be. I really hope I'm wrong. She studied my face. Blimey, she said. You look terrible. Are you well? She laid her warm hand on mine. I gave her a little squeeze. Momentarily I felt ashamed. Wanna come and eat with us tonight? she asked. I made an excuse. Oh, all right then, she said. Perhaps tomorrow? Suddenly I have an overwhelming urge to mother you. She looked puzzled when I said I couldn't make it this week. Well, you will take care of yourself, won't you? she said, and gave me a hug. Love you, I said as I closed the door and left her there.

I finished work early to do some shopping. I went into a shop where I'd only ever looked in the window before. It was all chrome and white inside. An impossibly fab-looking assistant with straight black hair wafted towards me. She asked if I needed help. For a moment I wasn't sure what she meant. Are you looking for anything in particular? she said, and smiled gently. I told her I wanted a drop-dead gorgeous dress. Something sexy and floaty if possible. No problem, she said, and took me to a rail of filmy, strappy things. They were swaying in a perfumed breeze. In the changing room a scented candle burned. The fragrance of freesias enveloped me. My underwear looked as chunky as something issued by the army.

The apricot and turquoise dress shimmered over my head and settled on my body, cool and so light that it felt like just-born skin. My breasts were held in the bodice like tensely ripe fruit. My shoulders gleamed unfamiliarly. I was dazzled by the dress. The black-haired girl appeared, and we looked at my reflection together. That's so totally you, she said to the me-in-the-mirror. Do you really think so? I said. I knew it was totally me. She showed me the matching sandals. Insubstantial straps and leather flowers. Stiletto heels. I had never worn shoes like them. It seemed to me that I hadn't looked at clothes properly before.

Once I'd started I couldn't stop. I bought a pair of low-slung cream linen trousers, and a scarlet and cream striped bustier. Another pair of high-heeled, pointy-toed shoes, and a tight little belted jacket with a huge tortoiseshell buckle. All these things were the sort of clothes the woman-in-the-ladies-loo-mirror wore all the time. They were no big deal to her. I paid with my credit card. The beautiful girl herself wrapped the clothes in tissue paper. I walked to my car and looked down at my old clunky shoes. How could I have bought them? They looked so sensible, so comfortable, so sort of square-shaped.

When I got home there was someone in the lounge. I ran in. I didn't recognise the boy watching TV. He had a shaved head and looked about twelve. I asked him who he was. A mate, he said, not taking his eyes from the screen. Who are you? He was bouncing a football as he sat watching the screen. I didn't know what to say. I asked him how he had got in. Back door, he said.

I went to the kitchen and locked the back door, then made myself a cup of camomile tea. I was shaking, but I only noticed when I tried to pick up my cup. Straw-coloured liquid spilled onto the table. I traced some patterns with it. After a while the boy appeared in the kitchen doorway with the football under his arm. See you, he said. I'm off now. He had a little whispery voice, as if he had chest problems. OK, I said. He left the TV on and slammed the front door.

I couldn't move. Gradually the way I felt about my house when the boy had been there eased off. I didn't feel like I was a visitor in my own home any more: someone who'd come for an interview, say, or for some unpleasant physical examination. It was my own place again. My welcoming, safe place. But now I was beginning to be afraid about how my house could change so quickly; one moment almost shutting me out, and then just as quickly drawing me in again. I didn't feel I could trust it anymore.

I got up stiffly; my legs were aching. I locked the doors, closed all the curtains and blinds, and went to have a bath. As I relaxed in the warm bubbles I heard someone at the front door. I stayed in the water. He called my name through the letter box. He said he knew I was there. Baby? His voice got louder and hoarser as he shouted. Baby? I really want to see you now! What's wrong? Are you narked off with me? He banged the door really hard. Then he went to the back door and tried that. There was a pause and he was at the front door again, banging and banging.

For fuck's sake, what's your problem? he yelled. Let me in, you bitch.

His voice sounded deeper than it did when he spoke, and ragged. I thought perhaps the door wouldn't keep him out. I pictured his curling blond hair springing away from his temples. The way his long legs stretched out on my white sheets. The intimate smell at the nape of his neck. At last he went away. I got out of the bath with difficulty. It was as if all my joints had seized up. In the bedroom I put on my old soft nightie, took some pills, and climbed under the duvet.

I have titanic dreams

I WOKE AND realised I had missed work. It was a long way down to the kitchen. I busied myself making toast. My limbs felt as if they were made of pipe cleaners, my bones long and thin with a covering of dry, puffy flesh. It was difficult to grasp my mug, to sit upright on the chair. The toast on the plate looked like a floor tile. I knew it was the medication. I needed to do normal stuff but I couldn't leave my chair in the kitchen.

Then I began to remember the dream I'd had. I had been sailing on an enormous, opulent ocean liner. At first I didn't recognise anyone. I felt completely alone on my journey. Nothing happened for a long time, people just drifted around the decks wearing beautiful clothes. And then we heard the boat was heading for a colossal iceberg; there was no escape. Everyone gathered on board. I remember thinking that this was only another *Titanic* dream; it was OK, and nothing was real. Anyway, things always turned out fine. No one ever got hurt.

But slowly, as we all milled around, quietly terrified, I began to recognise people. My mother and father were there. Alison and Tom. Even their children and the two puppies they had got for Christmas. Each child was holding one. My gran was lying on deck in her hospital bed. My boss was on the phone. I began looking through the crowd for someone very important to me, but I couldn't find him or remember what he looked like. Then we only had a few minutes left. The air was dazzlingly cold. The iceberg, emerald green and glinting in a powerful beam of moonlight, was getting nearer. I could hear it creaking, and realised it was making a kind of high, metallic, wordless singing sound. Its freezing breath rushed at us, spiking our lashes and hair with stinging crystals. In the moonlight we all looked dead.

I gazed down into the beautiful black water. Impossibly narrow, almost transparent fish with smiling mouths flicked about. Suddenly I knew that if we all jumped in together we would be safe; everything would be fine. I told the others what I knew. I went round the little crowd saying, just trust me, you have to trust me. Alison was fussing with her kids' hair. She was holding the sleeping baby in her arms. Even the puppies were quiet. My gran got out of bed and held my mother's hand.

We all kissed and said I love you to each other. My father put his arm on my shoulder and asked me again if I was sure. Yes, I said. We all clambered up onto the rail. They all jumped in together, but I couldn't move. I leaned over and watched them lying peacefully on the gently moving surface of the water. Without reproach they all gazed up at me as they floated down, and sank without struggling, their clothes billowing round them. I watched until they disappeared from view.

Then he was there with me. His hair shining in the moonlight. I thought that now we could be together. His blue eyes were strangely blank. Your turn, he whispered, and lifted me up. I tried to lock my arms round his neck, but he was immensely strong. He held me away from him out beyond the rail, and then he let me go into the dark, muffling ocean. The water was silent as I entered it, but soon I heard the ice singing to me. I remember watching him shrink as I drifted down and away like a piece of luggage. I tried to raise my arms to him, but it was too cold, the water too heavy for me.

I sat in the kitchen and tried to work out what it meant. I thought so hard it felt as if the shape of my face was changing. My eyes stretched and grew enormous, my head ballooned into a dome, but no explanation for the dream occurred to me. Just as I felt two stiff antennae breaking through the skin of my forehead it dawned on me. Maybe it meant I was too dependent on other people, and didn't trust him enough. I should have let him in when he came. I should have given him a chance to explain himself. I got up and did an inventory of myself in the hall mirror. I expected to see a girl with the head of a giant insect, but all was present and, if not correct, at least in the right proportions. Then, as I smoothed my hair back into place, I had another idea about the stupid dream: maybe it was totally meaningless.

I get lots of fresh air

I DIDN'T SEE him for twelve days. On the thirteenth he rang me at the office. Say you're ill, he said. I've got a plan. Leave work now. I looked across at Alison filing her nails. That may take a little time, I said. So? he said. I'll wait by your car until eleven, baby, no longer. Oh, and by the way, are you horny? Alison was watching me, her nail file poised like the miniature bow of an invisible violin. She raised her eyebrows. Yes. Yes, I am, I said. Before you leave take off your panties and put them in your bag, he said. I put the phone down extra carefully. God I feel terrible, I said. Suddenly I've got this totally splitting headache. I didn't fool Alison, but my boss seemed content. Don't do anything I wouldn't do, will you? Alison said. I could tell she wasn't joking. I stood in a toilet cubicle and took off my pants. Then I ran to my car.

We drove out into the countryside. Everything was sparkling, ridiculously beautiful. I wanted to ask about the strange boy in my lounge but I didn't want to spoil things.

He fiddled with the radio until he found something to please him. Then he leaned back and closed his eyes. I kept gazing across at him. Like what you see? he said after a while. He opened one eye and blew a kiss at me before settling back again. His hands lay in his lap, their backs lightly covered with blond hair. It still didn't seem the right time to talk about the boy in my lounge, or his own behaviour at the door on the same day. I decided to let it go. I reached over and rested my hand on his hands. He sat up. We're nearly there, he said.

We had lunch out in the garden of a pub by a river. Giant hogweed strode down towards the water. Two swans drifted by, beating their wings at each other. I thought they'd probably been together for years. I'd read about the faithfulness of swans somewhere. We were both hungry, and ate in silence. Just after the waitress had left the coffee, he started patting his pockets. Shit, I don't seem to have my wallet, he said, and lit a cigarette. Don't worry, I said. Little working girl, he said, and patted my cheek.

There were two women eating at a table with a sun umbrella. He stood up. Next part of plan, he said, and took my hand. We walked away from the women and round the side of the pub. There were nettles and dandelions. He positioned me to face the wall. He told me to lift my skirt up. I felt him pushing himself into me. I stood on tiptoes and arched my back. He slipped his hands up under my top and bra and pulled my nipples downwards. I couldn't help making a noise. He laughed softly into my hair. As he did it to me I watched the swans gliding round each other. I thought they might be in love. The pebbledash of the wall grazed my cheek. When he had finished he pulled me round and kissed my mouth. The women out there, I said, I can't walk near them, they must have heard me. It'll brighten up their sad lives, he said. And dragged me after him, past them to the car. I felt like a rag doll. In the car mirror I saw my cheek was bleeding. You look like a bloody wreck, he said. Sort yourself out.

At my front door I looked back. I thought he was coming in. He stood by the gate. Don't leave me now, I said. I'll cook you something later. You can relax and watch TV. He stood and tapped the gatepost, he was already turning away. No, he said. I've got stuff to do. He was gazing down the street. What sort of stuff? I said. He looked at me without speaking. Then he pointed his finger at me. You need to be very careful about that, he said. Then he walked away. About what? I called after him.

I believe that size matters

OVER COFFEE ALISON asked me what was going on. She said she had been worried about me. I haven't seen you for ages, she said. You can't stay on sick leave indefinitely. This is the second time in less than a month. It's that Mr Blond, isn't it? You're looking decidedly wan. And what have you done to your face? I tripped, I said. And I've had a urine infection; it's taking some time to clear up. I'm not surprised, she said. I nodded back towards the counter. I wish now I'd had one of those smoothies instead of coffee, I said.

Somehow I couldn't be bothered to explain it all. We just go out for a drink, nothing happens. If you ask me, she said, you're not yourself at all. You never used to lie to me. Don't you trust me any more? Also it's a very risky thing getting involved with claimants. I'm not involved, I said. And I didn't ask you. I stared into the froth in my cup. I suppose Alison was counting up to ten again. It took her a while. Perhaps it was twenty. I looked across at her. I'm sorry, I said. I don't know what to say. I felt utterly switched off.

We drank our coffees in silence, and listened to the conversation at the next table. One woman was telling the other about a mutual friend. You know she's had it all taken away, don't you? she said. The other, younger one didn't seem impressed. Well, it wasn't as if she had much use for it all, did she? she answered with a slight sniff. Alison and I stared at each other, trying not to laugh. Look, she said, getting serious, I know it's none of my business, but I think you should be careful. Has he tried anything? I pretended not to understand. Has he tried to shag you yet, I mean, she said. He's a claimant, for God's sake. He's just come out of prison. You don't know anything about him. I told her there was nothing wrong with being a claimant. Also, I said, he's paid his debt to society.

Now I know something's going on between you, she said, and banged her hand down sharply. The two women on the next table turned round pointedly, and stared at us. Got a problem? Alison asked them. Then she leaned towards me and touched my hand. I know I sound like your mother, but honestly, will you listen to yourself? Paid his debt? Are you mad? Look, I said. It's nothing. I hardly know him. I don't even like him. Mmmm, Alison said. I got up to get more coffee. Now I wanted to go on talking about him.

Alison was putting on some lipstick when I got back to the table. It was a new colour for her. She seemed to have decided to shut up about the burning issue. Actually, she said, talking about getting into people's pants, I've been feeling really sexy recently. Tom does as well, so that's handy. You know how rarely these things synchronise when you're in a long-term relationship. And having the kids around all the time doesn't exactly oil the wheels, so to speak. I nodded. Prepare to laugh: he's developed this mad obsession about whether he matches up, y'know, size wise. I didn't respond. I was thinking about the wall of the pub, other things. We drank our coffees. I thought you were having a smoothie, Alison said. Yes, I said, but somehow I forgot. And the smoothies seemed so sort of smooth. I suddenly wanted a roughie, do you know what I'm saying? God, yes, she said.

We went on sipping our drinks. Before I could think of something riveting to say she began to nag me. Tom says you should give this mystery man a wide berth, Alison announced. He says wait for someone steady. Tom says better to be safe than sorry. I put my cup down. How dare you discuss my private life with Tom? I said. What the hell does he know about passion? Tom with his packed lunches and Thermos flask. Bloody Tom with his extensive, colour-coded collection of bloody Simply Red CDs. What does he know? We both stood up. You stupid, stupid girl. You're having sex with this guy, aren't you? Alison said, far too loudly. Yes, I am, I said. And do you know what? He's got the biggest dick I've ever seen.

I eat colour coordinated snacks

I FELT REALLY bad about what I'd said to Alison. She was my one true friend. Somehow, though, it was too hard to make the first move. All weekend I was on my own. I don't know what I did to pass the time. Lots of grooming. Lots of smoothing and creaming and masking. I can say without exaggeration that my feet looked truly angelic. I tried on the new sandals I'd bought but not worn yet. I gazed at myself for hours, wearing my new things.

Eventually I realised I just looked stupid. Like a little girl dressed up in her mother's clothes. But not even cute. I folded the new clothes up in the tissue paper, put them in the cupboard, shut the door and left them in the dark with my ruined jacket. I lay on the sofa and ate Wotsits. I watched epic quantities of trash TV: botched cosmetic procedures, thirty-four-stone teenagers, gay blokes overhauling straight blokes, mentally disturbed dogs and their mentally disturbed owners, mad nutritionists who sniffed the poo of obese secretaries. It was all quite calming. I left a short message on Alison's home phone.

I turned the TV off and waited. I hadn't eaten anything but pseudo cheesy snacks all weekend. I'd drunk nothing but Lucozade. It was a fact that only orange stuff had passed my lips. I went on lying on the sofa and drifted off to sleep. I didn't hear Alison's call. The answerphone was blinking when I finally sat up. I dived at it. She sounded just the same, and she called me her little duck egg. I was to go to her house. Tom had taken all the kids over to his mother's.

I showered and threw on some clothes. On the way I bought red wine and a roast chicken from her neighbourhood deli. These I offered at the front door. Come here, you daft nit, she said, and hugged me and the chicken at the same time. I told her I was sorry about what I'd said. Tom had every right to his opinion. And that actually, of course, what he said was true. Also, although it was none of my business, I was sure he was more than generously endowed in the family jewel department. Stuff Tom, she said. I should never have quoted him like that. Anybody would think he was the fifth oracle. Well, I said, I did think it a bit strange, when usually you make such a point of not listening to anything the poor man says. Quite, she said.

We opened the wine and I started to eat the chicken. Alison didn't want any. She went to get something from the kitchen and I looked around her lounge. It was a messy room, but warm and quiet. There was a weathered-looking teddy lying across the back of an easy chair, and the Sunday papers were in a heap on the coffee table. I su¹denly realised how much I didn't know about her life with her children and Tom. It was as if she knew I needed her to be the same Alison I'd grown up with. If I wanted to go somewhere she was always available. Like now, for instance. Tom had taken the children out so I could come over to see her. I started to cry. What's the matter? she asked, appearing with a napkin and a pepper-mill in the doorway. Is your chicken so disappointing?

I love you, Alison, I said. That's all. Back atcha, she said, and wiped my tears with the napkin. I told her everything had gone wrong. I really needed to sort myself out. I told her I was scared of what was happening to me. Suddenly I knew it was true. It was as if I was spinning out into space with only a thin, fraying cord holding me to some enormous mothership. Come on, she said. Don't be so hysterical. So you've done some things you wish you hadn't. Get in line. Behind me, for starters. This is true, I said, sniffing.

Now, what we need is a small plan of action, she announced. The world has not come to an end because you have slept with some waster. Did he use a condom? Are you are on the Pill? Yes, and yes, I said mechanically. I just wanted her to stop. She scrutinised me. I'm not even going to go there, she said. That is so fundamentally crucial, I won't insult you by droning on about it. Right? No need, I told her, and smiled a calm, ultra-in-control sort of smile. She seemed to be look-ing for further reassurance, then she turned away and bustled about. Now, you mustn't see him again, that's obvious, she said, over her shoulder.

I sat with a piece of chicken in my hands and watched Alison. I felt as if she knew what to do. So you can come and stay with us for a bit, she offered. That'll help you get your head together. Then if he comes round you won't be there to be tempted by the bastard. I'm not sure he's an actual bona fide bastard as such, I said. She put her hands on her hips. You're not in a position to judge, my unbelievably naive but sweet young friend, she said. What is obvious is that you are very unhappy. Am I correct? Sexed up, yes. But unhappy also. Unfortunately the two seem to go together.

As she talked I began to feel sleepy. She ran me a bath. Go and have a nice soak, she said. I've put some of my magic everything-will-be-OK elixir in it. Then you can have an early night and get your stuff in the morning. She brought me a mug of hot chocolate and a gingersnap when I was in bed in the spare room. I was wearing a pair of her pyjamas. Now, can I get you anything else, madam? she asked. I pointed to a shabby book in the bookcase. Don't tell me you're going to wallow in *The Wind in the Willows* again? Yes, sirree, I said, settling back. This is my bible, you know. I'm off to see Badger. Find me a door scraper, and shut the door on your way out if you would be so kind.

I agree to things blindly

IT WAS LOVELY staying with Alison. Tom was so kind; he kept out of the way and took the children with him. They wouldn't speak to me after the bread incident, and I couldn't blame them. They were a bit implacable looking when we did meet. I told Tom he was a hero. Well, yes, he said, scratching his chin, I know. After two days I went back home; I couldn't stay very long. I didn't want to impose. When I got back I felt like Mole feels when he's abandoned his humble pad and gone off to live with Water Rat, then returns. There was my little house, with its mound of post on the mat, and its half bottle of souring milk in the fridge. It felt very quiet after Alison's.

My mother had left a few messages on the phone, but I couldn't be bothered to talk to her. I thought about sending a postcard, then realised that probably wasn't a good idea. I had to go into work for a meeting with the head of department about my mad sick leave. It went OK. I blubbed and told him some story.

In the evenings I did things people do when they're in their own home, like changing the bed and opening all the windows. I put the radio on, and bustled about, cleaning the kitchen cupboards and watering my gasping plants. I even made a big pot of soup so I could smell it cooking. I managed to eat some, but I wasn't at all hungry. It felt as if I was killing time, waiting for the real owner of the house to return so I could hand over the keys and leave for my other life.

I went back to the office and just kept going. Each day became a little easier, as if I were learning a new job. By the end of the week things felt fairly OK again. On Friday Alison and I were having a break at our desks when she said she had this suggestion to make. And that I wasn't to freak out or say no before considering what she had to say. God, I said, I promise, get on with it.

She said she'd met this bloke, a business friend of Tom's, and he was new to the area, really nice. Also good-looking. She and Tom thought he would be great for me. I didn't say anything; I just carried on sipping my coffee. So, she said, shall I set you two up on a date? I allowed a silence to develop. I hoped it would express how I felt. Well? Alison said, still smiling like some chat show host with a reluctant celeb – if there was such a thing – What d'you think? Hmmm? Are you completely mad? I said. Since when were you a match-maker? I told her the very idea of being set up on a date made me feel yukky. I knew you'd say that, she said calmly, but just think about it. I already know he's nice, it doesn't have to be a big deal. Just a drink, and then you could go on from there, if you want to. Or not.

Somehow I agreed. I remembered how kind Tom had been. How Alison wanted me to be happy, and I couldn't say no. Alison did the organising. The guy's name was Rob, which somehow didn't seem auspicious to me. I began to think about the term *blind date*. Why blind? It sounded horribly vulnerable-making and ordealish. Not at all fun and frivolous. I'd never been on one before. I began to regret saying yes almost immediately. I decided to check the guy out, get there early, and if he looked even remotely off I would run away. Tom and Alison could stick it up their bums, thank you very much.

I feel sick of visitors

BEFORE I EMBARKED on the potential fiasco of my date with wots-his-face I decided I had to do what the magazines call *build bridges*. As my parents and I lived on different planets, rather than opposite banks of a river, it felt like a tall order. So instead I went to do some shopping. There was no food in the house and I was tired of munching Ryvitas with Marmite. I'd even developed a small mouth ulcer, they were so salty and shardlike. And drifting through the aisles was always inspirational.

At the supermarket I realised it was simple; I would invite my parents for a meal. So I rang them immediately. I had to have something substantial and competent to offer. A proper roast dinner would convince them I was fine, and that they were fine and we were fine. I bought a big chunk of beef and all the usual trimmings. When I got my bags home the meat had bled all over the carrots and even soaked into a loaf of bread, which had gone pink and spongy.

It took me most of Saturday afternoon to get the meal ready. While I cooked I managed to drink nearly a whole bottle of red wine and at least one G and T. By the time they arrived I felt blurry and loose. When they came in I told my mother she ought to know straight away that the Yorkshire puds were shop-bought. Are you disappointed in me, Ma? I asked her. Have I let you down? Have I? She told me not to be so silly and pecked my cheek. Everything smells delicious, doesn't it, Daddy? My father didn't seem in a rush to take his coat off. He stood in the hallway looking serious.

Somehow I got it all on the table. My dad carved the beef. We talked about the weather and their garden. When we all had our heaped and steaming plates before us I began to feel sick. My mum was telling me about Gran. How she was sinking into a sort of gentle oblivion. I know, I said, and then I had to rush from the table. I made it to the loo in time. I tried to retch quietly, but some stuff got forced up my nose. I couldn't breathe. Mum and Dad were both at the bathroom door. I'm OK, I called, trying to sound upbeat. Something just went down the wrong way. I told them to go and enjoy their meals. They silently went back to the table. It all felt so sad I could hardly bear it.

I said I'd eat mine later, that I really only wanted a long, cool glass of water and some paracetamol. They didn't eat much either. That was all lovely, my mum said, when they'd finished. Where did you learn how to make those roasters so crunchy? From you, I suppose, I told her. I could see she was pleased. We quickly cleared up and then sat down with coffee and mints. I asked them if they wanted to watch some TV, but they didn't.

My mother took hold of my hands. Now, what's the trouble? she asked me. Something is obviously up. You have been avoiding us. Taking time off work. We rang Alison and she said you had been staying with her. And now here you are, pale and unhappy. Is it to do with your young man? She looked across to my father. He stood up and cleared his throat. We're worried about you, darling girl, he said. Come on, spill the beans. I picked up my cup. Nothing's wrong, my dear aged p's, I said. Just the usual ups and downs of life. You know how it is sometimes. Now, have we built a nice bridge or what? I asked them. They both looked at me doubtfully. They were so sweet.

We sat quietly in the lounge. I put one of their favourite CDs on. After all the cooking, the drink, and the vomming, I felt wasted. My dad began to snore gently and my mum got her knitting out. I curled up in the corner of the settee. It began to rain, and I imagined what the room must seem like from outside. The lamps glowing, three people looking at ease together. Just as I started to drift away there was a loud series of knocks at the door. It was as if each knock was a punch in my undefended stomach. I felt a thrill of fear radiate downwards from my head. I wanted to leap up, but I couldn't move. My father woke. My mother sat with her knitting needles poised. It's all right, I'll go, I said. But my

77

father was already up. Dad, I said, don't bother, it's probably nothing. He went out of the room. I knew who it was. There was a brief snatch of conversation, and then my dad came back in. It's someone for you, he said.

I wobbled out and shut the lounge door behind me. I felt the life draining from my heart, and yet I felt terrifyingly alive again. As if I'd been electrified. He was leaning against the door frame. Well, this all looks very cosy, he said, very nice. He said *nice* as if it was a swear word. A family get-together. He seemed about to spring into the tiny, airless hall. I'm really hurt, you know, he said, taking a leisurely drag of his cigarette. He seemed part of the wet, windy evening. Honestly, I doubt that, I said. Why would you be hurt? Because you didn't invite me, did you? he said, and laughed quietly.

I felt poised between the safe, well-lit room and the rain-soaked night outside. Me in the cold spotlight, standing like a wraith; like someone who never ventured outside. He with his body inclined towards me, one foot inside, his hair dark with moisture, his blue eyes cloudy, slightly blind-looking, already gone. The hallway briefly became the still centre of the universe. I could see trees thrashing behind him. I looked at the way his thigh strained against the damp denim of his jeans. Where've you been? Hiding? Wanna come out to play? he asked me, his voice soft and coaxing. I've missed you like mad. I lifted my hands and somehow pushed him out of the doorway. I felt his warm, thumping chest under my palms.

78

He smelt of wet pavements, alcohol and cigarettes. Get lost, I whispered. He was smiling. Don't think I'm letting you slip away that easy, he said. Just as I went to shut the door he leaned in and kissed me punchily on the lips.

I show too much

THE MEETING WITH Blind-Date Rob was in a pub on the
outskirts of town. Getting ready needed to be done at the
last minute. I slipped into my new cream trousers and the
bustier. They were a little loose because I'd lost weight. I
pulled the jacket on and stood in front of the mirror.
Something felt really wrong. Then I remembered the beautiful sandals. After I'd put them on I felt OK. In fact I felt like
the kind of girl who thought blind dates were a laugh a minute.
Then I nearly plunged down the staircase; I was unused to
the high heels. I told my reflection in the hall mirror that I
loved living on the edge.

I got a taxi to the pub because getting trollied seemed the
only way to approach a blind date. I always felt more fascinating when I was smashed. Anyway it gives you an excuse to
behave in new ways. I watched the streets thin out as we
drove. The sun was setting and all the little semis and bunga-
lows were drenched in a sort of Hollywood glow, the various

strips of lawn bright, bright green, as if they'd been touched up. There were people in their gardens, pruning, I supposed. Dogs on solitary walks. Each bus stop shelter I passed had a hooded group of boys scuffling inside. I heard an ice cream van. I began to feel the soggy, sluggish, melancholy feeling early evening can give you. In no time I was at the pub.

Rob hadn't arrived, so I ordered a double G and T and sat behind a pillar. They were playing that Jennifer Rush song about the power of love. Alison and I always laughed through it, but in the pub, waiting for Rob, it was like some sort of true cry from the heart. I started to feel like I might start sobbing, so I slugged down my drink and bought another.

I was still twenty sad minutes early, surely a total no-no in blind-date terms. I began to feel hot, then cold, then hot again. I must have looked wired, the way I kept taking my jacket off and putting it on again. I finished my second drink and just knew this was going to be a totally rubbish evening. I was at the bar when Rob arrived. I introduced myself. I'm not sure if we shake hands, he said. I told him I hadn't read the blind-date how-to manual. He had a nice laugh. He bought a bottle of red wine. We went outside and sat in the garden and began to drink.

So, Rob, I said. You're actually very handsome, aren't you? Did you know? Have you always been handsome? How does it feel? He wasn't fazed by my questions. He just laughed again and told me I was more than pretty. And how do you feel about that? We seemed to be getting on really well. The garden was end-of-Augusty, just the way I love a garden to be. The sedum was swaying around us in pink clumps, top-heavy with butterflies.

We talked for a long time, and he bought another bottle. You go ahead and drink, he said, I've had my two glasses so I'll drive you home. It got almost dark but we stayed outside. I told Rob I liked him. You can hold my hand if you so desire, I said. I'd drunk so much the plants and bushes around me seemed pulsing with energy, as if they were whipped by a silent storm. Rob was wearing really nice shoes. So much depends on that. His hair was black and he smelled woody. I asked him if it was time to go.

We walked to his car. I was weaving about, and Rob supported me. He felt slim but strong. He kissed me lightly, and it felt lovely, sort of airy and shy. I wanted him to do it again. When we got in the car I said, Why don't you just drive? He seemed surprised, and asked if I was sure. Don't you want me to take you home? he said. God no, I said, and stretched out. He drove into the countryside. The lanes got darker and darker. I'll tell you where to go, I said. Everything looked unfamiliar, but I made up directions.

Then we stopped in a car park by the side of a lake. The water was completely smooth, and full of starry reflections. It was eerily beautiful. We sat quietly and looked. Does it matter that we don't know each other? I asked him. Do you like me? I couldn't see his face properly in the dark, but I felt he was smiling. Of course I like you, he said. You're very cute.

Cute? I said. Is that a good thing? You're sweet, he said, and patted my knee.

Suddenly I didn't feel drunk any more. Or cute either. I thought about stuff I'd done. I told him looks could be deceptive. I s'pose so, he said. He sounded a little switched off. He rested his head against the back of the seat and we watched some big white birds unfurl like flowers and land silently on the lake. It was as if they were dragging nets of stars down with them. The dark water whirled and the stars stretched and shivered. I waited for them to firm up again. Then I started to take my new clothes off. They slipped off almost as if they were enchanted. My body looked startlingly white in the half gloom of the car. I could feel the moon's glow on my skin. I sat and waited for him to touch me. I closed my eyes so that I would feel even more naked. It was a fantastic sensation. I knew I looked amazing.

Nothing happened. Rob was resting his arms on the steering wheel, still gazing out at the lake. I shook his arm. Don't you want me? I asked him. I began to feel more than pathetic. Don't you like these, Robby the handsome Rob? I said in a stupid voice, and lifted up my breasts and pointed them at him. I could see they looked like two unappetising, sunken buns. I moved them about a bit; one pointing up, the other down, then vice versa. He turned and tried to focus on my boobs. What are you playing at? he asked quietly, his hands gripping the steering wheel. Put those away, it's too cold for them to be out. He settled back onto the headrest. God, he said, and sighed. You are so drunk. Then his hands slipped onto his knees and he closed his eyes as if he were about to fall asleep.

I felt as if I were disintegrating. I struggled to dress but I was shaking too much to do it properly. My bare bottom squeaked like a frightened mouse against the car seat. I shoved my bra in my bag. I put my pants on back to front. My clothes had lost their magical properties. The lake was blank, its surface corrugated with little waves. No stars. Rain started to thump against the windshield. Then he drove me home. Once or twice he tried to make conversation. The windscreen wipers grated against the window. A snake of laughter kept wriggling in my throat, but I swallowed it down. When he stopped I slammed the door and ran into the house. On the hall floor I screamed with laughter until I was paralysed.

I am a one-trick pony

I KNEW THAT weeks went by. The calendar said so, but I didn't feel them as days and hours, minutes and seconds. I felt them in my blood maybe, or my bones. I longed to see him. When I woke up in the morning the longing woke up too, like a strange cat on my bed. The feeling moved up from inside my pelvis and settled in my throat. That's where it stayed all day. I found it difficult to eat, even if I'd wanted to, with this thing in my throat. Then I began to worry it might go away. It was as if I carried him around with me somehow; his springy blond hair and beautiful feet. The soft fuzz in his groin. His neck with its jumping pulse. The flavour of his spit. And the smell of his cool, even-coloured skin like some buttery, crushed herb.

At the same time if I closed my eyes I played out another, idiotic blind-date version of myself in a moonlit car, waving her empty tits around in circles. And another lay motionless on the hall floor, dribbling onto the carpet. I even saw myself out on the ruffled waters of a lake, surrounded by silent, hovering white birds, raising a glass of red wine to the rain. Why had I been there? Whom had I been with? I found it hard to recall how long ago it had been. Everything was blurred, leaching into something else, painfully punctuated by encounters I didn't understand. I know I managed to get to work almost every day. But I didn't know much else.

Repeatedly I relived the early summer meal by the river. The way he had gripped my breasts with his hands, the electric current that forked downwards into my belly when he had pinched my nipples and pulled them hard. I remembered the giant hogweed craning in on us. I cringed when I thought about how my cheek had scraped against the rough wall of the pub, the sounds I'd made in the hot afternoon. The two women, motionless under a faded parasol, poised with bread rolls, holding cutlery. Listening, listening.

Alison started bringing sandwiches into work for me; I didn't have anything in the fridge. The supermarket seemed like such a complicated place. Instead of going out and sitting in the park for lunch we decided to use the staff canteen. Everywhere I looked people were cramming chips into their mouths. What's with all this manic chip-eating today? I asked her. Is it just me, or is there some sort of contest going on that we don't know about? No idea, ducks, she said. Who cares anyway? Let them all choke. I want to know about your blind date. It's been a while, and you haven't even mentioned Rob's name. Rob who? I said. Has he been in touch with you or Tom? I asked. She shook her head.

My throat contracted, or something inside it expanded. Alison gave me a look. Oh, it was all right, I suppose, I said. Alison stopped chewing her celery stick. Do you know that thing has negative calories in it? I told her. Mmmm, OK, she said, we'll talk about him some other time. Who? I said. Rob, you dreamy twit, she said. And for God's sake, eat something.

The afternoon stretched ahead like one of those sick-making family car journeys. Are we nearly there yet? I mouthed across the office to Alison. She just stared at me and went back to her computer. I sat at my desk and tried to look busy. I couldn't do much anyway. All the paperwork looked like new, more difficult versions of the stuff I usually worked with. Our boss left early, and we all relaxed.

Alison and I sloped off to get a coffee. Some women from another section were in the kitchen, and Alison seemed to know them all. They were talking about a television programme. Everyone was really into it. Alison was the most knowledgeable. God, Alison, I said, when did you start to care about stuff like this? Everyone stopped talking and started to listen to us. Believe it or not, Alison said, this is the real world. She was smiling at me. TV, magazines, stuff like that. It's how we bond in the workplace, love. Over trivialities. It's known as communication. Comprondayvoo? I do watch TV, you know, and films, she told me. I even listen to music when I'm not with you, believe it or not.

There was some giggling. Then someone I didn't even recog-nise, a woman with open pores all round her nose, said if you asked her I'd always been on another planet. I stared at her. She was wearing a smiling silver dolphin on a silver chain round her neck. Its eye was picked out with a tiny green stone. I thought how creepy that was, when you really analysed it. She's just a little dark horse, that's all, someone else said, and leaned over to mess up my hair.

I looked at Alison. She was holding her cup to her lips, but I could see she was smiling at me. A little dark pony, maybe, she said. I couldn't think of an answer. They all looked so together, there, making drinks, chatting about stuff, giving their opinions. Suddenly I felt them all shoot away until there was a huge empty space all round where I stood. Then, faintly, I heard someone start talking about how much weight they'd put on, and they all turned their backs and joined in. Alison was in the thick of it.

I went off to the loo, but really I was bored with the whole loo thing. It was like I was spending all my life in there. Still, I felt it was my space. There was someone in a cubicle, so I had to wait until they had done everything they had to do, which took ages. To pass the time I swished my hands around in a basin of cold water. Eventually the slow woman came out, adjusting her skirt, which is always so irritating. As she washed her hands, she looked at my bluish fingers floating in the water, and then at me in the mirror. Are you all right? she asked. Why? I said. Are you? What were you doing in there? Writing a love letter?

Finally the loo was empty. I made sure all the taps were

shut off, and then I wiped the surfaces with a wad of paper towels. I was thinking of being a dark horse, or pony maybe. I remembered a time when I was little and my mother and I tried to call some horses over to talk to us. She sat me on a stone wall, and waved a droopy clump of especially succulent grass. They may come, she said, smiling at them as they stood in a self-contained, leggy group in the middle of the field. Suddenly, as if they'd agreed amongst themselves, they broke apart, wheeled round and thundered towards us.

As I sat on the sun-warmed wall I thought they would soar over my head and gallop up into the sky. I thought they might take my mother with them, and leave me alone on the edge of the field. It felt like magic, the way they slowed and stopped in front of us. They stood and kindly ate the grass my mother offered, although I knew they didn't need it. I sat with a horse either side of me, and breathed in the smell of bruised grass, muscles and hair. I imagined each huge heart with its maroon tubes and valves. I patted each solid, springy flank as it moved against me and felt its warmth, its horsiness. As I gazed into a tender, blackly brown, wise eye, I could see myself floating on its liquid surface. I ran my hands over each silky, quivering nose, and breathed in the sweet breath from inside. And then they were gone. They were dark horses.

I dried my hands. They were so cold it felt as if I was touching another person's hands. I looked at my reflection and thought my eyes looked more like the eyes of some small domestic creature. Perhaps a hamster's or a rabbit's. Or the eyes of the last unsold kitten in a cage at the market. A kitten that understands the truth about the waiting, brimful bucket and the stallholder's strong, competent fists.

When I got home I dug out his phone number. I tried to keep it simple and low key. I tried not to sound needy or tearful. I put a CD on so that he would hear it in the background and think I was a normal girl. Someone who had decided, on impulse, to ring a guy she thought was nice. I left a voicemail asking him to call. I suggested we meet for a chat or something.

I gather at the river

IT WAS THE end of the third week after I'd left my message. Just as I thought I would have to ring again he got in touch. He didn't say much. If you want, he said, when I suggested we meet. I spent a long time getting ready; it was important to strike the right note. I wanted to look gorgeous, irresistible, eatable even, and not as if I'd tried too hard. It was a tough one. But after messing about in front of the dreaded mirror for half an hour I was unhappy with my make-up. My eyebrows looked like two wrong words someone had tried to scribble over with a black felt-tip pen. One was higher than the other, which made me look like a joke chef in a cartoon. My cheeks were way too pink, and my eyes were starey; haunted somehow. I washed it all off and started again. It was safer to go down the 'no make-up' make-up route that all the magazines were talking about. When I'd finished it looked as if I wasn't wearing any. But not in a good way. My blank canvas was still blank. I wasn't sure if I'd failed spectacularly, or it was a startling success. I told myself if you had to ask, then you knew the answer.

I drove to the pub in town he'd said he'd be in and waited outside for him to appear. As I sat in the car I listened to a whole episode of *The Archers*. I watched the pub door repeatedly open and close. Each time it opened I thought it was him, but it wasn't. On the radio two old, posh agricultural people were making love. *The Archers* had changed since I used to listen to it in the kitchen with my mother. The sound effects were so real I felt embarrassed, and all the love action seemed to be occurring on horseback. It was difficult to decide who was huffing and puffing, the lovers or their mounts.

Just as the closing music came on he got in beside me. I couldn't say a word. He filled the car with the smell of beer and cigarette smoke. I revved the engine madly and shot off. He asked me if I was OK. I nodded. I couldn't look at him. It was as if my eyes were locked on the road. He put his hand on the back of my neck and massaged it. He asked where I was taking him but didn't sound at all curious. I told him to wait and see. Fine, he said. I don't care where I go. I had planned a walk by the river. I wanted to make things more ordinary; more like other people's relationships. It seemed like a good idea to take him to one of my favourite haunts.

We parked the car under some pines and started off. I began to explain to him how I felt about the river, and he listened, smiling. He said he had places he felt like that about. I stopped and looked at him. We were holding hands. The river was behind him, the evening air leaf-sweet and cool under the trees. He gazed steadily back at me. It felt like a miracle, as if I'd caught something everyone had warned me was dangerous, which instead was gentle; as if something wild had calmed down. You are beautiful, I love you, I said. I wasn't sure if I'd spoken the words out loud or if my heart had blurted them silently.

He didn't react, so I repeated them loud and clear. He smiled and put his arms round me. I could feel his gorgeous, strong heart thumping. I burrowed my head into his neck. I felt as if my spine were turning into a rippling, honeyed liquid and I was about to slide down his body into a pool at his feet.

We walked again, holding onto each other. Along the riverbank we passed people with their dogs, parents helping their children learn to ride bikes. He was quiet and relaxed. I kept my arm round his waist, and he rested his arm round my shoulders. Everything was so lovely. I could see how we looked together. After a while I asked him if he was having a good time; I'd begun to think he might be getting bored. But he didn't answer me. I don't think he heard. I started to feel jumpy and nervous. I had that feeling you get when something is slipping away, and you can't stop it. Like the light on a short winter afternoon. I needed something to happen. I thought probably he was being nice because he was going to dump me. His arm on my shoulders felt dead. I started to think he didn't want me any more.

It was getting dark, and the little bats that live by the river began to flit about like animated leaves. It was always a sad time when that happened. We stopped by the bridge and looked down at the water flowing fast and smooth, the same colour as the sky, but full of sparkling streaks. We watched the sky turn a creamy cerise that slowly leached into the water. As we stared at the river it began to look weird: solid and slow moving, silent and muscular, more like dry sand than liquid. I pushed my hands into my pockets and found a sweet. It must have been there a long time. He turned away from the water and looked at me.

In the half-light he looked unfamiliar. The sunset made his skin glow and his hair paler. He still looked like his other, good, gentle self. The one I didn't know. What have you found? he said. I held up the squashed sweet in its ragged paper wrapping, and he took it from me. These used to be called Opal Fruits when I was kid, he said, do you remember? Then he put it in his mouth. We stood on the bridge together and he held me tightly. Here, he said, kissing me, open up, and pushed the warm gooey sweet into my mouth with his tongue. Strawberry! I said, but really I felt as if it was a little chunk of him, and I could eat it. He hugged me to him. I wanted to stay on the bridge, out there, suspended, but I knew that was stupid. It was dark now, and the river beneath us held onto the last glow of the sky.

Gradually I realised I was gripping him so tightly my arms were trembling. I told myself to chill out, it was obvious the moment had passed. He wasn't responding to me any more. I let my arms drop. I wasn't surprised when his phone shrilled, the little screen shining bluely. Yeh, he said, yeh, yeh, OK. Then he listened for a moment. Nothing important, he said, looking at me without recognition, concentrating on his conversation. Yeh, mate, you fuck yourself, he said, and laughed. Pick me up in, say, ten minutes at the usual place. No probs. The blue light died. Without it the evening felt pitch black, the trees along the sides of the river bent over.

Gotta go, babe, he said. But it's dark, I said, and a long way to the car. So? he said. You're a big girl. He was already walking away from me. I started to cry. Don't leave me, haven't we been having a nice time? I called. I couldn't help myself, even though I knew it would make him angry. He strode back towards me and grabbed my shoulders. Nice, he said. Nice? Shut the fuck up about nice, and pushed me away from him so hard I collided with the railings of the bridge. Suddenly it seemed essential I make him stay. Like some sort of test I had to pass. I'm sorry, I could hear myself shrieking, I'm really sorry. I didn't mean to make you mad. Please don't go.

He came back towards me, his footsteps resonating on the wooden bridge. I thought he was going to do something, hit me perhaps. Instead he wrapped his arms round me and kissed my forehead. Don't cry, he whispered. I didn't mean it. You'll have to get used to the fact that I'm a cruel bastard.

He wiped my tears away with his warm hands. No, you're not, I said, and kissed his cheek. Then he was gone. I stood with my hands glued to the metal railings and strained to hear him running away until I couldn't hear him any more.

I do some double-talking

FOR FIVE DAYS I didn't go out. I ignored the phone and erased all messages without listening to them. God, that tiny winking eye! Like some creepy uncle at a family party. Anyway it seemed as if I'd reached some place – a precipice or something – where I needed to think. What was this problem I had with men? Why couldn't I be a regular girl? But mostly the questions were unaskable. Just long, confused rafts of why? And how? And why not? I sat for hours in front of the mirror, gazing. The mirror was on the inside of the wardrobe door, so I had to prop it open and look, perched on the end of the bed.

I was fairly pretty, cute even, and that was the truth. Sometimes I really liked my reflection. Hey gorgeous! I said. Or I asked, affectionately, questions like, What's your problem, lovely one? And, Who rattled your cage, you bird of paradise, you? Or even, but this was early on, So many people would kill to have your life, you ungrateful girl, go and stand

99

in the corner. I looked at myself from all angles. Everything was groovy. Everything was in its proper place.

I remembered watching some intense woman on a morning TV chat show talking about *strategies to aid self-knowledge and subsequently move forward.* So I got my hand mirror and looked between my legs. Hello, I said, greetings. The whole enterprise seemed a little heavy, so I tried to be jaunty. Who do you think you're staring at? I joked. The thing didn't blink. It certainly didn't talk back. I opened it up a little, though I felt squeamish. Then I got spooked; it seemed so sad and angry. The whole area looked like a punched eye. I thought I detected a look of reproach. In the end I whispered, Goodbye and good luck. I felt we both needed that. Then, at the last minute, quickly, Have a nice life.

I was feeling hungry all the time. I stocked up on the things I wanted to eat: lots of meat, like Mia Farrow in *Rosemary's Baby.* Chicken and chops, sausages and burgers. Big slices of ham, each piece hanging out of my mouth like the tongue of a camel. Faggots like lumps of roasted brain. I ate everything in front of the mirror. It was amazing how stupid my face looked when I chomped. I vowed never to eat in public. How could the people I'd eaten with keep a straight face? Or even prevent themselves from sicking up? God! I was glad I'd had this opportunity. I could at least save myself that embarrassment ever again. Drinking wasn't much better. As I sipped my face looked simultaneously wounded and emotional. And nauseatingly pious, as if I'd been insulted for my faith and might break down. But this was all good, I thought: self-knowledge, and then the moving forward thing.

I decided it would be interesting to conduct an experiment. You know, go over to the dark side. So I stopped combing my hair. This was a big concept for me, and really out there. The stunning thing was that as the days rolled on and my hair got wilder and wilder, it began to look better and better. Why had I ever bothered? My slavish attachment to straighteners suddenly seemed insane. The new look was more grown-up. More don't-fuck-with-me-ish. Even a bit rock-chicky. The messiness said something to the world. I felt like maybe I was a dangerous bitch, someone very temperamental. Someone men would fall passionately in love with.

It was a joke, of course. And I told the mirror, So who are you kidding, you loser? I knew I had to get tough. Get out of your bedroom, you adolescent twit, I shouted. You with your bird's nest hair and your horrible vulva and your stupid, stupid chewing! Nobody likes you! You can't even stand yourself! (I said everything with an exclamation mark attached.) Take a long, hard, honest look at yourself for once! The portion of my room reflected in the mirror was so impoverished, so drab, so totally full of aloneness, it pierced me to see it.

I gazed at the discarded plate of bones on the bed next to me, the straighteners on the floor, and I cried with complete abandon. Me-in-the-mirror and I cried bitterly together. I felt for her, she felt for me. But even as I blubbed I knew I would have to stop soon. I swear that once, after a sobbing bout in which I cried into my hands like someone in a Victorian painting, I peeped out through my laced fingers and she was greedily watching me with the faintest of smiles on her face. The second she saw me looking she dropped her shaggy head and started bawling into her cupped hands again.

I sat up and hiccuped. Why doesn't he love me though? I asked her. Why? Why? It felt comforting to indulge in repetition. I sounded like someone in a play. Why? She shook her head slowly and shrugged, miming one of those haven't-got-a-clue faces, which was surprisingly annoying. Perhaps he does, I suddenly thought. Perhaps he does, and he can't show it. Perhaps he needs me to help him. She looked sceptical. And also maybe you should get lost? I said. Honestly, what do you know about anything? You miserable, insincere cow! In a flash it occurred to me. Maybe he'd been trying to tell me something. Perhaps he wanted us to move in together, something huge like that, and he found it difficult. That's why he'd been a little touchy. It made sense. I reluctantly glanced in the mirror. My reflection had her hands over her ears and her mouth open.

I got up and slammed her into the wardrobe. There was another mirror on the outside, and things looked much better in it. I showered and dried my hair. Then straightened it to a luxurious shine. I rang Alison and we chatted. Her voice sounded faint, as if she was up on the surface of the ocean and I was down on the seabed in a submarine, but it was lovely to speak to her. She wondered if I would do a favour at short notice and mind the baby. I asked if she really wanted me to be sole carer for another of her children, after the bread incident. That wasn't your fault, she said. You can take him out for a nice walk in his buggy; he'll be asleep the whole time. I won't be long. It seemed like an excellent way to get back into the real world. Though I didn't say this to Alison.

I indulge in retail therapy

MY HOUSE NEEDED sorting out. The baby probably wouldn't notice, but it didn't feel right to have him in a sad, dishevelled place. And who understands what babies see? Maybe everything. Maybe we all start off very wise and far-sighted and end up stupid. Anyway I was worried the invisible, dark mood clouds swirling around might get to him. So I opened the windows and pushed the vacuum around, sucking up more than dust and cobwebs. I picked some rice pudding-coloured dog roses from among the undergrowth at the bottom of my garden. Their open faces looked like gentleness realised. They had the frondiest of leaves, and when I sniffed them they gave me the most honeyed, creamy distillation of rose I have ever known. I put them in a sage-green bowl and they arranged themselves perfectly, the leaves spraying out in perfect collars around each flower.

I had lunch because when the baby came I didn't want to think about things like that, then I sat in the kitchen near the roses and drank some tea. The warmth in the room and the flowers' fragrance made me feel drowsy; sort of heavy and thick-tongued. I rested my head on the table and drifted off. The doorbell rang and I leaped up and ran down the hall. There was Alison, a bit breathless, and the lovely baby in his buggy. So, I'll see you at five, she said. You've officially saved my life, and pushed the buggy up over the doorstep whilst handing me a bag of equipment. It's a good afternoon for a walk, she called back as she got in her car. He loves a walk. Then she was gone and the baby and I were alone in the silent house.

In the kitchen I had a good look at him. Crikey, I told him, you are the most scrumptious baby I have ever seen. He smiled kindly at me, and sighed, looking around calmly, his pudgy hands resting like two pink cakes on his lap. He seemed to be interested in the roses so I picked up the bowl and brought them near him. He laughed and grabbed at them, then let out a sharp and shocking scream. I dropped the vase and it smashed, spraying water over his little brown legs. He stiffened and started bellowing.

His tiny hand was still closed round one of the rose stems and I realised with a razor-sharp slice of fear that all the thorns on the spine were hurting his tender palm. I burst into tears and sat beside him in the spilled water. Somehow I forced him to open his hand and took out the strangled rose. I got cold water and bathed his palm, singing to him through my tears. He quietened and watched without malice as I soothed his hand, shuddering rhythmically.

Everything had gone wrong and I'd only been in charge of the baby for ten minutes. I kissed his head and tried to look at his hand again, but he wasn't going to allow me. Little boy, I said to him, I'm so, so sorry. His cheeks were shiny with tears and I gently wiped them. I felt as if my heart would break, he was so sweet. I emptied the bag Alison had left and found a cup with baby drink in it. He drank it all. I sat on the kitchen chair and shook. Inside it was as if I had emptied out, like a cloud after a downpour. I wondered how to explain to Alison about his poor hand. Little man, I asked him, would you like to go for a nice walk?

I pushed the sleeping baby in his buggy through town. The wind barrelled round and round the concrete walkways. I went in nearly every shop. They were all playing the same music. The shop assistants were dusting shelves and rearranging things, talking about their weekends: . . . *anyway, he said, then I said, then he said, then I said* . . . lowering their voices when I passed by. Girls, girls, girly girl girls, I wanted to say, as if I give a damn what he said and you said. All the shops were empty; I didn't see one single, other shopper around. It was as if the real people had been spirited away. I concentrated on keeping the buggy moving, otherwise the baby might wake up.

There were lots of lovely things to buy. I wanted a scarf patterned with blobby circles; a pair of caramel leather sandals; some chicken marinating in olive oil, chillies and garlic; a dusty, plaited loaf of bread; a long Cossack coat with a fur collar, but I didn't want to disturb the baby. In a department store I decided to stop and sit down; my legs felt decidedly dodgy. The café was empty, and the food looked artificial. I ordered a cup of camomile tea and perched on the edge of the chair, rocking the buggy. As I drank I worked out how much time was left till five o'clock.

In the home furnishing section they were going for an oriental theme. I wondered why people would want to decorate their homes that way. I touched all the curtains and picked up vases and candlesticks. In the lift going down I detected the faintest of stirrings from the buggy, so I rushed out of the shop and started to run. Only when I reached the underpass did I slow down. The lights were dim and I could smell wet concrete and maybe urine. People had daubed messages on the walls. One, written using red gloss paint read: Is this fuckin all? I wanted to get the baby out of there quickly, but it was difficult; I had to manoeuvre round a warped trolley.

As I emerged into the bright light I stopped. There were some things on the cover of the buggy, things I knew I hadn't bought: a candlestick and a little Chinese cushion. Silky, emerald-green tassels dripped from each of its corners. An embroidered dragon or bird or reptile, I couldn't tell, stared up at me, its eye a sparkling blue gem. The colours glowed in the gloomy mouth of the underpass and seemed to undulate over the creature; it looked as if it were about to take off, hightail it back to the department store and tell security.

I was so shocked I felt winded. The path ahead was deserted. The wind gushed out of the underpass and sent my hair upward in a swirling cone, pushing me towards home. I walked as briskly as I could whilst still looking normal. When I got there I rested against the front door for a little while. I left the still-sleeping baby in the hallway and carried the things into the lounge. I arranged them on the coffee table. Then I sat on the sofa and looked at them, waiting for Alison to come back.

I get tied up once in a while

I WAS SUMMONED to the head of human resources' office. He wasn't someone any of us knew very well. It was the first I'd heard of him. I had been hoping, when I gave it a thought, that no one had noticed my slightly spasmodic work attendance over the past months. Obviously I had been wrong; these people notice every sad little thing. The room was in a part of the building I had never seen before. I walked slowly up this weird corridor, reading all the names on the doors until I found the right one. It occurred to me that he could just be an actor, someone they employed for the day to do interviews with rubbish employees. I knocked and entered. He looked the part anyway. Sit down, he said, and went on shuffling through a file. He read it for so long I thought it must be about me.

I checked everything out. No photos on display, just one of those stupid pens jammed in a holder stuck to the desk like a thrown dart. Yep, it all looked like a stage set. There were shelves and shelves of ring binders full of Health and Safety information. God, I thought, the poor bloke must be so bored, but then I remembered the day job idea. It was a way of earning some dosh. Finally, because I felt he was overdoing the file-reading sequence, I was forced to ask him if he found the story of my life interesting. He looked up slowly. The story of your life is of no concern to us, he said. Believe me. And this, he held up the file, is not about you. What we are concerned about is your productivity, or lack of it.

He talked a lot – blah, blah, blah – and I sat there blinking. Honestly I could actually hear myself blink. His shoes looked like enormous wholemeal pasties. His socks had little pink pigs on them. And then I realised he was expecting me to say something. So I said I was sorry, that I had been involved in some big family problems. I told him if he read the records properly he would find that I had an excellent attendance record up till now. Well, that's not strictly true, is it? he asked, and smiled mostly with his lower lip. Excellent is not the word we would use if we were being accurate, is it? So I babbled on about everything being resolved. I told him I was now back on track. We all hope so, he said, without emphasis. Because as I said at the beginning of this conversation, this is your first official warning. Then there was more blahhing as I backed out of the office. Thank you very much, I said as I closed the door. Maybe it had been a real interview, I thought.

In the loo Alison told me I should be careful. You don't

112

seem to understand, she said, after I'd explained my idea about the actor/head of department/stage set thing. You may lose your job. Then what? Dunno, I said, but chill. I told her she worried too much. Everything will work out, I said. It always does. Actually, babe, she said, sometimes it doesn't. Has some alien entity sucked your tiny brain out of your earhole while you slumbered? She seemed really down. Are you angry with me, Alison? I asked. Have I said something to piss you off? You poor, clueless thing, she said, of course not. All I'm saying is, for starters, stop missing work. Just promise me that at least.

Suddenly I felt scared. I felt myself shrivelling. Now don't cry, you silly noodle. She sounded brisk, like a teacher handing out one's pitiful maths test results. Just sort yourself out. She gave me a tissue, then took it from me and wiped my face. Honestly what planet are you on? Planet-I-don't-think-I've-got-a-hope, I said. Well, come back to earth, she said, and gave me a hug. You really are a full-time job at the moment. Am I? I said.

It was lunchtime so we went to a café in town. I couldn't find my purse so Alison bought me a bowl of soup and a roll. Now, she said, spooning hers into her mouth, I want to see you eat all that up. You are getting too skinny. I told her I couldn't seem to do stuff any more. Yes, you can, she said, breaking my roll in half and smearing butter on it, you just have to concentrate. And eat. Alison didn't seem her usual self to me. I sense you are being a little unfeeling, I told her.

I'm struggling, you know. Yeah, well, life is hard, ducks. We all struggle. This is tough love, she said, dunking her bread. *El Tougho Luvvo*, baby. That's what I think you need. Everybody does.

I stood up, but kept my voice low. Since when did you have all the answers about what I need? I said. Everybody? Who's everybody? I could hear my voice getting louder. You and Tom and the children-from-hell? Those clueless, moustached, pot-bellied, female drones in work? I shouted. God, I thought, bloody Alison. I watched her as she sat there, hoovering soggy blobs of bread into her mouth. I s'pose the baby told you what I need as well? I asked her. Then I wished I hadn't mentioned him. He was entitled to his opinion.

Whatever, she said, waving her hand languidly, still smugly munching. Alison, I told her, you don't know shit. I felt good saying it. Then I walked away. She called after me; there's really no need to explain to me about the baby's injuries, or apologise. I'm sure you didn't mean to, as usual. Oh and thanks for the candlestick and the little cushion thing though; *très, très chic*. I came back to the table. Obviously gifts are wasted on you, I said. But then I had to tell her how sorry I felt about the darling baby. She didn't say it was all right though, just went on slurping her disgusting soup.

I drifted through town thinking how ungrateful Alison was, how she didn't understand me and my situation. Probably because my life was so strange and exciting, and hers was so, well, bland and uneventful. But at the same time I knew I didn't understand either, that recently I'd felt like a punctured balloon darting about at a party I wasn't even invited to, making a slightly embarrassing sound. So really, how could Alison have the answers? I couldn't blame her for losing interest in me. I was boring myself into a coma. It was all so tiring. I knew I had to go back to work, but I held my phone and waited. I was just about to send an abject apology to her when miraculously he sent me a text; just an address and the word NOW after it.

I ran to my car and drove. I felt ultra-alive as I dodged the traffic. Then I was at the entrance to an expensive-looking block of flats. He buzzed me, and I stood in the carpeted lift, silently flying upwards. He was waiting, and I ran into his lovely arms like a girl in a drippy, romantic novel. I started telling him about Alison and the meeting, but he kissed me. Forget that dreary bitch, he said, and the fucking personnel wanker. Both losers. Come in. The flat was elegant, with huge windows. Outside clean-cut seagulls hovered and banked. It's fabulous, I said. Is it yours? I remembered the grotty house with the smashed window. You and your little, tiny, picky questions, he answered, and playfully tapped my nose. What would you like to drink?

I chose Baileys. I wanted something sweet and comforting. I sniffed the creamy liquid. Come on, drink up, he said, wandering around, his bare feet leaving indentations in the thick carpet. OK, so, first, it's way too light in here, he said, and he went to a control panel and fiddled. The curtains closed. I was sorry the seagulls had gone. Now we can relax and get drunk he told me. Do you agree? I said yes, I did.

The Baileys was warm, I could feel it spreading through my bloodstream, travelling along each limb, making my legs heavy and fuzzed up. Unkinking everything. One lamp glowed on a small glass table. He sat back on the huge suede sofa. Take off those disgusting tights, he said, relax. I propped myself up on the cushions and he took my feet in his lap. He looked all creamy and gold in the lamplight. You have beautiful feet, he said, and kissed them. He massaged the arches and I lay back and closed my eyes. Keep drinking, he said. The aching, frozen area between my shoulder blades melted. Instead it felt as if something warm and heavy were tumbling down my spine.

After a while he told me to take off my clothes. He told me to stand in front of him and do it. My clothes all slipped off. He gestured for me to give them to him. He held my knickers and buried his face in them. You'd better have a shower, he said. He was drinking whisky. I drank again from the heavy glass he'd refilled for me. I was entirely in his hands. You can do whatever you want to me, I told him. I know, he said, and led me to the bathroom. He helped me into the shower and turned it on. He adjusted the temperature of the water. Now wash yourself properly, and don't forget your hair.

I splashed all sorts of gorgeous things over myself from the row of bottles on a glass shelf in the shower area. The hot water, the alcohol, the perfume in the shower mist, being with him, sent me somewhere. As I turned off the water I heard music coming from the lounge. I was drying myself when he came into the bathroom. He peed in the sink, and then told me to get back in the shower. You can wash me now, he said. I poured something from one of the bottles over his shoulders and began to soap his chest and belly. He had a scar, still slightly red, that looked almost like a flower just below his ribs on the left side. A slight altercation, he said. When I touched it he pushed my hand away. The crown of my head came up to the level of his nipples. I sucked them until they stood out. He kept his eyes closed and sipped from his whisky glass. It was so wonderful. And my cock, he said, and smiled.

We dried each other and chose perfumes to put on. He led me into another room off the bathroom and sat me in front of a mirrored dressing table. Then he dried my hair, brushing until it clicked with static. His body was wet and evenly coloured, almost unreal. I'm good at doing this, he said, and wound my hair into a thick coil. He used it like a rope to pull my head backwards. I could feel my neck being stretched taut. Try to swallow, he said. You can't, can you? I watched his reflection in the mirror. He laughed softly and held his erect penis, moving his hand up and down the shaft. He let my hair go and squeezed my breast until I screamed. That feels fucking great to me, he whispered. Tell me how you feel. Shall I do it again? He stood behind and held my breasts. Then he twisted them in his fists. I could feel his penis between my shoulder blades. Tell me when to stop. But I didn't. You bitch, he said. Are you coming already?

I loved watching us in the mirror. We looked like people in a film. Now I want you to wear this, he said, and tied a silky mask over my eyes. Is that OK? I felt peaceful with my eyes covered. He led me back into the lounge and helped me to sit on what felt like a dining chair. He positioned my arms and legs. I'm using your tights to tie you, he said. I could hear him ripping them. I felt him wrapping the flimsy fabric round each ankle, and winding it round the chair legs. He pushed my knees apart. Are you comfortable? Try and move. Now I'm going to tie your hands behind your back. Have another drink. He held the glass to my lips, and as I drank some dripped onto my raw breasts. I told him my arms hurt, but he didn't answer. Are you going to fuck me now? I asked. Questions again, he said and slapped me short and hard on the side of my face. I won't be long.

I waited. Jazz was playing, music I didn't understand. I felt absolutely alone, and aware of everything around me, my body weak and slack. But somewhere inside my ribs, or pelvis, I was intensely clasped and trembling, almost in pain. Then he was back, and his mood had changed, I could sense immediately. His hands were shaking, his breathing quick and shallow. I told him I needed the bathroom. He pulled my hair as he took the mask away. I felt as if it had melded to my face, and he was peeling my skin off. I kept my eyes shut.

Have you taken something? I asked. Not fucking now, he

said. Christ, you're not going to fucking chat, are you? And pushed my balled-up knickers into my mouth. I stayed perfectly still as he began to do things to me. Tears slipped out of the corners of my eyes. I could hear him grunting. He hurt me, but I didn't make a sound. I didn't look at him at all.

Then I felt him untying me. He was breathing quickly. He made me lie on the floor with a cushion under my hips, and took the little wet bundle out of my mouth. He stood above me, and I forced myself to look at him. His body was shiny with sweat, his ribs standing out, stomach slack. His jaw seemed wrong. In the corners of his mouth were little spots of foam. Only the whites of his eyes were visible, and I was sure he couldn't see me. I said his name but he didn't hear me. He was holding a shiny black dildo in his hand. I could see his erection had disappeared, and he was trying to activate it again, muttering to himself. He kneeled down between my legs. Scream now, and I'll kill you, he said. I swear to God I will.

There was a hammering sound. Someone banging at the door, but it felt part of what I was feeling. I couldn't tell. He leaped upright as the lights snapped on. There were two men in the room. I lay on the floor with the thing he'd used still inside me. One of the men lunged and punched him, but he hardly swayed. The three of them stood poised, looking at each other. The other man said, I told you not to come here any more, you bastard. He stood between them, naked, then he put his arm round the man who'd punched him and pulled him near. He was laughing and dancing on the spot. Don't ever do that again, he whispered into his hair. The two men seemed wary of him. Then one of them nudged me with his foot. What's this, you naughty boy? he asked. Nothing, he answered. Then they started laughing loudly, and went into the kitchen. I heard one of them telling him to get his clothes on. It sounded as if they were starting to cook something. After a while he shouted to me. Get up, he said. Your taxi will be here in five.

I don't talk to the animals

THE TAXI DROVE away. Then I walked up my garden path.
The house was just the same. For a while I couldn't get my
key in the lock. I stood outside and checked I was in the
right street; perhaps this was not my place. But then the key
turned. I let the door swing open. There was a message on
the answerphone. That was the first thing I saw; my ridiculous answerphone on the hall table. On-off, on-off, on-off. I
watched the red light blinking like a third, faltering eye.
Although I knew, it took me a while to work out what the
tiny light meant. Red was for danger, surely. Or pain. I didn't
have the strength to listen anyway, so I drifted past and stood
in the kitchen.

I thought how sweet the kitchen looked. The things I'd
bought. It made me laugh. I felt as if all my bones were
broken into gravel; my whole skeleton crushed to pieces of
shale. How was I standing upright? It wasn't possible. And
yet I was. The amazing broken, unbreakable girl! If I'd had

the energy to jump up and down I'd have probably sounded like a box of dried peas. Here were my nice things I'd gone out and chosen. It was tragic really. I picked up my kettle and remembered how, after I'd got it, I kept on filling it with water and switching it on. Just to hear that cute whistle. Like the sound a nana's kettle would make in the kitchen of a plump, biscuit-baking nana. My reflection in its shiny surface showed me with a huge, pendulous nose and minuscule squinty eyes. Ravishing.

Something terrible has happened to me, I whispered, standing in the kitchen. It was like a film set. Obviously the kitchen of a nice woman. I could see her darling children arriving home from school waving their A-grade test papers. Hungry for homespun, vitaminy meals. And then her muscly husband. Maybe he'd bend her over the sink and push his huge schlong up under her pinny. Shove, shove, shove, and *kerpow!* Her glossy hair would swing softly. All the time she'd be stirring something delicious on the stove, maybe even feeding the hamster. But stop, I thought. Who cares about that stupid woman? I have experienced something very bad and serious. Surely something horrible and wrong. Or maybe it was wonderful. I couldn't tell yet.

Then I began to sense a soft, pink balloon of pure happiness grow in my chest, so I sat down and laughed until it drifted up into my head. This balloon, it was like a barometer, and I knew it showed me things. So I concentrated on the way it moved to fill each hollow and shelf inside my skull, and while that happened I watched the evening lower itself into the garden. Through the kitchen window I could see my wrought-iron table and chairs quietly standing on the patio. A slim, grey cat I'd never seen before leaped up onto the table and surveyed the garden, then turned to look at the house. I wondered if it saw me. I hated that cat sitting on my table, its smug face, but there was nothing I could do about it. Beyond the cat I could make out, at the end of the lawn, my cream roses like miniature lamps amongst the tangled, darkening hedgerow.

On the horizon the hills waited for the evening to reach them. I knew my house was closing in around me, like a slowly shutting, plush-filled shell. And I would be the skin-less creature curled up inside. I could be safe in here. Then I felt a cold breeze flowing in from the hall. I ran to the front door, it was yawning open. How had I left it unclosed? How could I have done that? It was a thing I never did.

On the front step the grey cat sat upright staring at me. Shoo! Get lost! I shouted, but it didn't move. Its eyes were the colour of pale green grapes. The cat and the sky over the houses were exactly the same colour. Maybe the cat was the evening, come to bless me, help me rest, I thought. No, that couldn't be right; I had always been afraid of cats. So I pushed it with my foot, not hard, just firmly, but it still sat on, gazing. I slammed the door and locked it. Then I bent down and peeped through the letter box. The cat was walking away up the garden path, its tail twitching. As I crouched, watching,

I felt bereft; I'd denied a harmless animal shelter. Didn't that mean I was a really cold person? Now I wished I'd asked it in. Given the poor creature some milk maybe. It would have been lovely to listen to it purring, coiled round my legs on the sofa.

I lay down and covered myself with a blanket that was usually draped over the back of the sofa for decoration. I turned on the TV and switched channels. It was incredible, on every programme they seemed to be talking about me. Some aspect of my stupid life was being examined. The pictures they showed didn't look like me of course, but I knew what was going on. I reckoned they must be desperate for material. Serious, bearded experts were giving their opinions. Mostly they made good points. I felt myself drifting off under the warm blanket. It felt as if the grape-eyed cat was vibrating against me.

Then someone was banging on the lounge window. I thought it might be him. Come to say he loved me. I stood up. Whoever it was had their hands pressed to the window, trying to peer in. But it was dark in the lounge and I was invisible. I crept to the front door and listened. Someone was standing at the door. I could see them through the mottled glass, talking to the person who was making all the noise. I realised it was my parents, and I let them in.

What's happened to you? my mum asked, but she didn't really seem to want an answer. They were a bit agitated. My dad said that Gran was ill. That they'd come to take me with them to the hospital. I picked up my coat. I think you should go and spruce yourself up a bit first, dear, my mum said. Change your clothes, sort your hair out. We don't want you scaring the horses.

As I trailed up the stairs I could hear my mum asking where the kettle was. I wanted to rush back down and shout at them to leave my kettle alone. To get out of my house, and take their stupid string bags, fucking bifocals and dreary matching fleeces with them. I felt beyond all that shit now. Soon I was going to leave them far behind. No real rush, darling, my mum shouted up to me. I'm sure Gran will be all right, don't you worry. She usually is. I'll bring you a cup of tea, and maybe a little sandwich? She was opening and closing cupboards as she called to me. Or a biccy? Bang went a cupboard door. I know, I'll make you a nice boiled egg and soldiers. You always like that. I dropped onto the top stair and started to cry quietly. I loved the sounds coming up from the kitchen; cups rattling, drawers opening, my kettle's whistle. Yes please, Mummy, I called to her.

My timing is dead on

I SAT IN the back of the car and listened to my parents. They were deciding on the best route to the hospital. I had a fierce headache, and their soft conversation was like a light rain falling on the hot roof of my head. I held onto the door handle and made sure my seat belt was on. The fabric of the seat was coarse and warm. I ran my hands over as much as I could reach. I wanted to feel really there. Really with my parents in their neat car with the tin of icing-sugar-covered fruit sweets in its special place on the dashboard. I wanted to laugh out loud at the idea of that tin of sweets.

What's going on there? my mum asked. Just checking your car out, I said, and settled back, trying to think about my grandmother dying. Maybe she'd already fallen off her perch. It was funny. There was a time when I would have been hysterical at the idea of her death. Now it felt like an item of news I'd heard on the TV. Something that was happening to someone I didn't know in a foreign country I would never go to. I nearly got out of the car when we stopped at some traffic lights; I had so much to sort out.

It felt wrong though, not to care at all. I tried to whip some feelings up but the inside of my chest was as hollow as an empty rubbish bin; totally, absolutely dried up, with my poor, tiny heart lying at the bottom like a crushed coke can. The more I thought about it the more desolate the scene became. No, not a bin, more like a vast sheer-sided sinkhole. Halfway down I could make out seagulls twirling. Their demented screams spiralled on the uprushing air. I started to sob. My dad looked at me in the rear-view mirror. Poor sausage, he said, I know you loved your gran, but she's more than ready to go. It's time. My mother craned her head back at me and nodded, scrunching up her eyes. Oh, so that's all right then, I said. And you two psychic ones would know. I suppose you decide when to pull the plug as well? There now, he said, you're very upset, it's understandable. I saw them glance at each other.

As soon as we got inside the hospital I started to feel sick. The fag-smoking, hard faces of the nurses, who'd never fooled me; the sick people in their hundreds of rooms, breathing and oozing stuff onto their sheets; the warm air heavy with dead skin cells. I thought about the lines of trolleys full of sickening luke-warm food trundling up and down. And the sluices clogged with all kinds of gross lumps. I had to force myself to follow my parents down the endless corridors to Gran's ward.

I counted six beds, all occupied. Everybody looked dead as far as I could tell. One bed had the curtains pulled round. I could see a group of people through a gap sitting silently. It took ages for Mum and Dad to get chairs, and then we gathered round Gran. Her body barely made a shape under the blankets. I asked my mum if we were at the right bed. Don't be so silly, she said, holding Gran's hand. I wasn't sure. It didn't look like her. This one's nose was far too big. And her mouth looked unfamiliar. She was wearing Gran's rings though.

There was a small, elegant-looking man sitting in a winged chair opposite us. He had thick, startlingly white hair, brushed back into a mane. I couldn't help looking at him. One leg was crossed over the other and his arms were lightly resting in his lap. He smiled and nodded at me. Stop looking around, my mum hissed. Honestly, we're here for Gran. I tried to pay attention, but nothing was happening. I wasn't sure whether to breathe through my mouth or my nose. Neither felt safe.

There was a flurry from the group behind the flowery curtain. And a strange, guttural, obscene sound, accompanied by sobs and murmuring. Someone rang a bell, and two nurses came running. They looked as if they'd been eating chocolates, I thought. Don't look, mum said. The curtains heaved and bulged as if someone were having a fight inside. Then there was a huge, impossibly long burp, then silence. The nurses reappeared, and tidied their rucked-up uniforms. He's gone, they said to the ward in general. The elegant old bloke nodded and smiled as they went out. It's a mad house in here, I said. The whole situation is doing my head in. I've got to get some fresh air. Stay right where you are, my dad said. He pointed his finger at me. Not everything is about you. I didn't say a word, but I felt that was a touch harsh.

Hours went by. We drank tea. Gran was moving her lips and plucking at the bedclothes. My mum tried to listen. I asked what she was saying. Just the usual chicken sounds, I'm afraid, Mum said. She always loved chooks of course. I remember her telling me. She stroked Gran's cheek, nodding and smiling exaggeratedly at her like people do to babies. Kept them as a child, didn't you, Mum? she bellowed. My dad put his arm round her, and they both peered at Gran. Poor old duck, he said. Which I thought could have confused her, when she was so into chickens.

The old man still sat in his chair, looking noble. I couldn't help watching him. He didn't seem at all ill. He began to get restless, moving around in his chair, and laughing quietly to himself. He saw me looking, and gestured for me to come over. At first I thought I would ignore him, but he looked so sweet and smiley I stood up and walked across the ward.

When I got quite close he grabbed my arm and pulled me down to his eye level, uncrossed his legs and pointed to his crotch. Big brown stains were growing. Something liquid but heavier than pee plopped onto the lino near my sandal. The stench was stupefying. Almost visible. Billowing over me. My eyes watered, and I began to gag. I tried to call to Mum and

130

Dad but they were both leaning in over Gran. The old man laughed as I wrenched my arm free and ran into the corridor. I threw up my boiled egg and soldiers as I dashed to the toilets.

I stayed in there as long as I could, splashing cold water over my face and neck, then washing and rewashing my hands. I took my sandals off and dry retched as I dunked my feet in the sink; the old man's shit was splattered on my big toe. I crunched and swallowed some mints I found in my bag. I had a long sit-down on the loo. I really needed to wee but somehow I couldn't. It was burning and painful down there. I knew I needed to sit in a cool bath and attend to myself properly. I wondered if I was bleeding. My boobs were tender. Eventually I walked back to the ward. Someone had cleared up the sick in the corridor. The curtains were drawn round Gran's bed. I went inside. Where have you been? my father asked. She's dead.

I pour cold water on events

I GOT COMPASSIONATE leave, so that was a bonus. Though the idea of the bloke with the pig socks and pasties being compassionate made me want to scream with mirth. The funeral was OK. Lots of people I didn't recognise milling around at my parents' house. Plenty of alcohol and sausage rolls; what's not to like? But I couldn't concentrate on the buffet. I caught glimpses of Alison and Tom, which was nice, though somehow I couldn't get near them. I began to feel people were deliberately keeping us apart.

The best thing, I found, was to walk slowly in circles amongst the crowd with a full glass and a heaped plate. That way no one bothered you much. Lots of people still hugged and kissed me, even so. The usual suspects; old male friends my parents probably kept under the stairs, and wheeled out for special occasions grabbed the chance for a grope. I couldn't blame them really. They told me my gran had really loved me. That she'd been proud of me. One grotesque individual, as he cradled my buttock in his gnarly old hand, actually told me I was Gran's ray of sunshine. I couldn't help laughing. Mostly I didn't know how to arrange my face, so I just pretended to cry. That sent them scarpering.

Finally I bumped into Alison, and we sat on a bench in the rose arbour, perfectly bosky and cave-like. The roses had grown up and over the top. Pale pink blooms drooped down on us. The smell was intoxicating. It was cool and secret. Your parents' garden is so fab, Alison said, and linked her arm through mine. Pity one can't say the same about their ghoulish friends, I said. Some of them are nice, actually, she said. I told her that inside these funny old hedges it was as if nothing bad could ever happen. Even as I said it I knew it wasn't true. Well, yes, but unfortunately, not true, Alison said. It ought to be true, but it's not. That's one of the things I love about Alison. The way she says things I'm thinking. There hadn't been very much of that recently. Alison, I said, you are so wise and lovely. I know, she said. Can we be friends again now? I asked her. We always are, you nit, she said. Then she asked me how I was. I'm not your mum, she said. It's just that I worry about you. Nag, nag, nag, I said.

I was horribly restless. Who are you looking for? Alison asked. Only you keep craning your head round. Really? I said. That was surprising and scary; why was I doing that? What else was I doing that I didn't know about? I looked at Alison with her sweet funeral dress, and her shiny hair in its usual ponytail. There was so much to say, but also nothing at all.

Anyway, given it was my grandmother's funeral, I couldn't really tell her anything. It didn't seem the right time. I started playing the game we'd played since for ever. I knew she wouldn't be able to resist, and sure enough soon we were sniggering, quoting snippets of cheesy songs to each other. Perhaps we should stop giggling, Alison said. Behave, young miss. This is a funeral.

We decided to walk round the garden. I wanted to check out the runner bean wigwams. We agreed that vegetables were nice and grounding. I remembered the last time I'd visited. I could almost hear the ice tinkling in my mum's gin and tonic. I had fallen asleep on the bench near the bronze fennel. There was that moment with the mint, when I'd felt as if I had been pulled back from something. There you go again, Alison said, pointing at me. You're doing it now. I don't know what you mean, honestly I don't, I said. You seem weird to me, she said. All strung up. Who are you expecting? Mr Nobody maybe, I said. Alison decided to go and find Tom. She said she would see how my parents were.

Some people started to leave. I went up to my old bedroom and lay down on the bed. In the top drawer of the side table were my diaries. I pulled them out and began to read. I seemed to have been meticulous in recording all the school dinners I'd ever eaten. There were lists of birthday and Christmas presents, lists of the books I'd read, and the interminable walks I'd gone on. So boring and sort-of sweet. And lots of pages in code. I knew what they were about. Not sweet at all. Very boring though, and a bit pathetic, as those things usually are. I put the diaries back. Had I always been stupid? I fell asleep.

When I woke it was evening. I could still hear murmuring outside. I tottered down to the garden where some more people I assumed were close friends of my parents were sitting round a table. Alison and Tom were there. A parasol blossomed, its frilly edges fluttering. It all looked quite jolly. They had obviously been drinking for some time. The soft sunlight glowed in each pink glass. Having fun? I asked my mum. Someone found me a chair and I joined them. They were talking about summer holidays. Everyone was chipping in with lovely memories of happy times. Even the most boring remark sent them all into fits. I watched a tiny, dishevelled bird pecking at a crisp. Its wiry claws made a whispery sound on the metal table. I could feel tears blooming in my eyes; the little bird was so happy there with his meal. I was glad the bird didn't care about us. It put things in proportion. So I chilled out and drifted, drinking cold wine. I began to feel blissful.

There was a commotion near the back gate. Someone was shouting. It sounded like my father, which was unusual. Tom and two other men from the table got up, and went towards the noise. Mum strained to see what was going on as I poured myself another drink, then she looked at me, gesturing with her glass. Are you going to tell me who that might be? she asked me. Then she turned to Alison, and let out a loud gulping sound. We don't know what to do, she said into Alison's shoulder, her daddy and I are out of our depth. I think she was crying. Alison put one arm round her and gave me a look. Slop went her wine over the pin-tucked bodice of Mum's M&S blouse. Is all this something to do with you? she asked me. Maybe, I said, and gulped some wine, turning towards the struggling men. He broke through the little cartoony cluster, and ran headlong across the lawn, falling at my feet. One of his flip-flops flew off. My dad walked slowly towards us, trailing a jumpy, spouting, garden hose.

Apart from the snaking pipe and the hiss of the water there was silence in the garden. Everything else was motionless. I looked at Alison but somehow I couldn't hold her gaze. What's going on? she said quietly, reaching across the table to gently shake my arm. I couldn't answer because there he was, sprawled on the grass looking perfectly at home. I've come to get you, he said, grinning. His T-shirt was wet. I shrugged Alison off, and turned to face him. He sprang up and executed a perfect handstand. I couldn't help clapping.

Surely my dad didn't spray you, I said, as he lightly turned himself upright again. I could hardly speak I was so limp with laughter. My father coiled up the hose and shouted, Yes, I bloody well did, then held the nozzle up like a gun. I felt sorry for my poor old pa, with his forehead red and sweaty, his sparse hair tufty. At the same time it was all hilarious and exhilarating. Why did you do that, Dad? I asked. I did it because this person is not welcome here, he said, more quietly this time, and pointed the hose again. And now I want you to tell him to leave. It would be for the best, I think.

My mother made a wheezy, sobbing sound. She was still at it. Soaking Alison's best dress. Chill out, Mum, I said. Why can't you ever be happy for me? It's not as if anyone's died. She jerked upright in her chair. How could you? she said, in an odd, strangled voice. You poor, selfish, stupid girl. But I was already touching his beautiful damp hair, connecting with him again. It seemed to me the garden was suddenly filled with birds and butterflies, petals and flashing rainbows. And rooted to the ground all these stiff strangers dressed in black. God, what a crowd of absolute zeroes, I thought. How did you know where I was? I asked him. Sssh, he whispered, holding his finger up to his lips, I have my ways. Are you coming?

I provide bed and breakfast

I COULDN'T SLEEP. But that was nothing new. It seemed to me I hadn't slept since the late nineties. So I lay on my side, hugging the little nobbly pillow I'd brought back from my parents' house, and watched the dawn slowly bleach the curtains. I was paralysed by this creepy new mood, some new feeling that at its top end felt like utter exhaustion. For hours my brain had refused to move out of a circle of linked ideas I didn't want to think about. I saw a series of pictures clicking around like scenes from a shaky, antique film someone had projected on a grainy wall.

I could hear him breathing. One beautiful leg was hooked over me, both arms were flung above his head. I inched round and studied his armpits; the tiny coils of golden hair were almost like shells. I sniffed him. Then my scalp stretched, my stomach contracted, and I finally understood all the pictures I'd refused to look at in the night: I was terrified. That was it. The thought of him waking up made me pant like a cornered dog. I must have looked unhinged, craning round, dribbling, my hair electrified.

I don't know; maybe I fainted. When I opened my eyes again the curtains were a solid block of light. He was leaning over me. I need a slash, he said. Then a nice shag. When he got back into bed his penis felt wet against my leg. He asked me if I liked sex in the morning. It was a question I couldn't answer. One, because I didn't know, and two, because I was too afraid to speak. What's the matter, baby? he asked, and kissed me gently on the lips. I began to feel better. I hoped he hadn't noticed my eyes bulging out of my skull like a mad witch's.

You feel so stiff, he said. Relax. He massaged my back and legs until I spread out on the mattress. Soon I began to loosen up. That's better, let's be gentle, he said into my neck. You'd like that, baby, wouldn't you? I turned over, curled my arms round his shoulders and squeezed him tight. I told him I liked things to be gentle. Me too, sometimes, he said, and buried his face in my pubic hair. Don't, I said, but he wasn't listening. He pushed his tongue inside me. I love these little folds, he said. I wanted to knock his curly head away, but I didn't like to. Fuck, that's tangy, he said, and kissed me again. I didn't like his lips on mine; it felt wrong to be tasting myself. You've got to learn to love it all, he said, and laughed so cutely I had to join in.

It was surprising how much I wanted him to stick his thing in me. I grabbed his penis in the end, and guided it. We

rolled around and I loved how we felt together. How everything mingled. At one point I saw myself in the dreaded
wardrobe mirror, looking soft-cheeked and wobbly mouthed,
my eyelids shiny. What an idiot, I thought. One minute ready
to run away from the big, bad wolfy, the next romping with
him in the freaking forest. Even I could see how mixed-up it
was. Sick, even. I don't know anything, I told him jerkily, as
he rotated his hips between my legs. Nor me, he shouted.
Now stop talking, for fuck's sake.

When I woke again it felt like afternoon. He could have
been a slumbering angel; forehead completely smooth, feet
quiet, lovely fingers curled. I kissed him all over his face and
mouth. His penis was a floppy pink mushroom, nestling
amongst the undergrowth. I flicked it one way, then the other.
He didn't stir. I climbed out of bed, and had a shower. I felt
optimistic in the bathroom. But that may have been down
to my mint and rosemary shower gel. I read the label; it promised to lift the spirits. Still, there's something symbolic about
a shower, I've always thought, and part of that is watching
the used-up water schlooping down the plughole. From my
shower cubicle I looked through the small window I'd opened
to let the steam out. I could see blue sky with the prettiest
white clouds imaginable, and vivid birds looping the loop,
like something from a Disney film.

I decided to make breakfast for us. I left my hair wet; the
dryer was so noisy. When I tiptoed back into the bedroom
to get my robe he was lying in the same position, and I

covered him with the quilt. Then I tiptoed out. The atmosphere in the bedroom was different. I remembered my rock-chick-and-mirror period. How desperate I'd been then. What was all that about? I couldn't remember now, though at the time it had seemed the end of the world.

On the landing I noticed two supermarket carrier bags he'd thrown into the spare bedroom. I went in and shut the door. Then I emptied the bags onto the bed. I was scared he'd come in so I quickly went through the whole lot. There was nothing of any interest; just jeans, tops and pants, cheap toiletries. I fingered everything, looking at the labels, going through the pockets, and realised I was looking for something that wasn't there. Something that would give me a clue about who he was. I shoved everything back into the bags, and went downstairs to make breakfast.

As I cooked bacon and made the coffee the thought of him lying asleep upstairs felt good. This was what people did, surely? Had a lazy morning making love, taking a shower, having breakfast in bed. The rest of the day was a puzzle though. What else did people do with their lives? The smell of cooking, the sizzling and bubbling, felt so everyday I decided not to worry. I looked out at the table and chairs on the patio. No one had ever sat out there, except that cat, that one time. Maybe things would change now. We could have barbecues, with friends coming over. Alison and Tom and the kids might come. I even imagined him with a pinny on, cooking burgers.

I was putting things on the tray when he appeared at the kitchen door. I made you breakfast, I said, obviously. He drank the coffee in one go. Then scratched his head and yawned. I could see he hadn't showered. Never eat it, he said, makes me heave. He held out his hand, and said, Car keys? I heard myself tell him where they were. I need a vehicle sharpish, he said, and picked them up as he opened the front door. I ran after him.

Something told me to be quiet – I even clamped my hand over my mouth – but I ignored it. Where are you going? I squeaked. Something drove me on, even when I saw his face darken. When will you be back? I'm going to ignore all that, he said. Seeing as you've been so nice about the car and breakfast and all. And there I was, standing on the doorstep, holding a spatula, listening again to the sound of him going away.

I'm at home to Mr Truthful

I SPENT A few hours sorting the house out. I changed the bed and washed the sheets. It was nice to see them dancing around on the line, just like they did in other people's back gardens. In the kitchen I tried not to look directly at things. I hid the bacon and eggs. The coffee grounds clogged the sink, and that worried me. I dressed with care, and put plenty of slap on; as my mum always said, You've got to keep your end up, because no one else will do it for you. Outside I was dazed to see my car was missing. For a split second I even thought I should call the police. Then I went to the supermarket on the bus and bought stuff. It was quiet there in the evening. Lots of traumatised-looking women drifting around. Perhaps that's what we do: food shopping.

I ended up in the café, drinking thin hot chocolate. I read a magazine. There was lots of shit about relationships, and how to do great sex, great homes, great food, great children, and really great holidays. God, I could feel my own wonky ideas about how to live seeping out of every pore as I read. It was as if they were talking about life on some other almost-identical-but-not-quite planet. Not the one I was existing on anyway. There was nothing about what to do when you were afraid to go home. Nothing about that particular problem anywhere.

I waited for thirty-five minutes before the bus came. It was late when I got back, and the house was in darkness. No messages on my phone. I had to force myself to turn on the lights. Everything was in its place. I locked all the doors and shut the windows. Then I ran a bath. I poured in something that made the water a sludgy shade and slid into it. The steam in the bathroom smelled like vanilla, like delicious ice cream. I could feel the water softening me. I sang a song to myself and the taps plinked in time. The water quivered, and I realised it was because I was trembling. I was listening so hard I was actually trembling. I went to bed with some pills.

The next day I remembered to go to work. I threw my clothes on, called for a taxi, and practically ran out of the house. Miraculously I knew what to do at my desk. It was as if I'd switched to auto mode. Alison ignored me all day, which was fine by me. I felt as if everyone was ignoring me. By mid-afternoon I realised it was probably because I was invisible. Or only visible in a certain light, like those pale brown moths that fly out of a favourite jumper. Eventually it began to get to me, and I went to the loo to cry. Someone came up to my cubicle as I was silently howling and knocked on the door. It was Alison of course. I recognised her sensible shoes. I could have kneeled down in the lav and kissed them. Come out, she said. I need to say some things to you.

I washed my hands, and told her to get on with it. Come here, you, she answered sweetly, and put her arms round me. I rested my head on her shoulder. I told her I wished she was my mum. No thanks, she answered, and held me away from her. You are a nightmare child. I feel sorry for your parents. I didn't care what she said, just so long as she was talking to me. She folded her arms. Do you know how upset they are? she asked. How Tom and I feel? Do you have any idea how horrible it was when you flitted off after the funeral fiasco with that vile man? So many squealy, spiky questions. I didn't have any answers. Your mother is ill with worry. She'll cope, I said. She always does.

She was silent for a while, just sort of staring at me and shaking her head. So are you just going to stand there and tell me what a bad person I am? I said. Don't you think I know that? Lovey, you're not a bad person, she smiled, just a mixed-up, self-absorbed one. You always have been, admit it. Shit, Alison, I had to say, you're such a disgusting head girl. I'm actually feeling as if I might throw up just listening to you chant on. I felt something break loose inside me. If we were into home truths, why not? I thought. I began to see how it was, how it had always been. Alison was one of those types who loved to sit on the sidelines of someone else's fascinating life, and shout advice at them. She fed off me, and I let her. It made people like that feel even more smug about themselves when they could observe another human being struggling. Unravelling, if they were lucky.

I must have said all that out loud, because Alison took a sharp breath and said tearfully, If that's how you feel then there's nothing else to say. She sounded like a second-rate actress in a daytime soap. I almost laughed. You know where I am if you need me, she said. Then she walked out sniffing. I rummaged in my bag for a comb, but my vision was blurry. I splashed some water on my face, and blotted it carefully. When I looked in the mirror I seemed to have grown younger. I could have been my own little sister, only I didn't have one, thank God.

Alison's not my friend any more, I said out loud to the echoey loo. It's official, I now have no friends. Even my parents hate me. I watched my silly smile fade in the mirror. As I combed my hair I thought maybe it was all part of the scheme of things. I had to grow up sometime. No one really understood. They all thought they knew what was best for me. I had started a new chapter. I was living with a man, for holy Saint Ikea's sake. I was moving on. I was cooking stuff in my kitchen at last. Someone was occupying the empty side of my double bed. I felt equal to it all. But round the back of my little heart I could hear a lonely breeze whistling away everything I cared about.

I have red letter days

HE DIDN'T COME back and he didn't come back and he didn't come back. For the last couple of weeks I had been spending loads of money on taxis. I missed my car a lot. I fooled everybody at work. It was amazing. On the outside I looked like myself, and I sounded like her. I ate what she ate. I wore her clothes, although some of them I didn't like. I even put her make-up on. But inside I was just sloshing about. It made it awkward to use my computer and answer the phone, but I managed. I didn't know how much longer I could keep things going.

I felt as if some wet substance filled my cavities. It could have been water, it might have been blood; some sort of disgusting broth anyway. I was surprised my colleagues couldn't hear it lapping around as I stalked up and down the corridors. For all I knew I was leaving liquid splodges on the office floors. My vital organs had been sucked out. Inside my skull sat a microchip and some circuits. Inside my chest nothing at all. Not even an empty Coke can.

Alison was nowhere to be seen. I asked the dolphin neck-lace woman I'd always made a point of ignoring. She smirked, and told me how surprised she was I didn't know Alison was on leave. Gone abroad somewhere. But Alison doesn't like abroad, I said. She hates paninis. She likes Skegness and buckets of tea. Whatever, she answered, brushing dandruff off her acrylic jumper. That's all I can tell you. I could have slapped her stupid face. Well, I'm unimpressed, I said lamely; you haven't a clue, have you? and sloshed away.

I toyed with the idea of phoning blind-date Rob. He was the only other person in the world I knew. But after I'd walked myself through our meeting I remembered certain things: drinks in a garden; a ride through dark lanes; the pockmarked lake, a squeaky car seat; his white knuckles gripping the steering wheel; and finally that naked girl convulsing on the hall floor, and it didn't seem such a stunning idea. I felt sorry for him. How could the poor boy, with his nice shoes, have known that he was going to take weird little me out? And he'd doused himself with such nice perfume. Just as if he was going out on a common or garden, straightforward, pleasant, snoggy date. Let that be a lesson to him.

Every day in my lunch hour I went to the hole in the wall and took some money out. I liked seeing the little wad of notes in my bag as I travelled home on the bus. Systematically I cleared out my accounts. It gave me such a buzz. It became the highlight of each day. When I got home I would push it in a kitchen drawer. Finally there was enough. I already had something to put the money in. It seemed right to use the red treasure box I'd had since I was a little girl. Then I'd used it for my secrets. I'd loved that it had a lock and key. Now I started to look for somewhere to stash it. The garden seemed like an ideal place; it was somewhere I felt safe, somewhere only I visited. I stood on the patio and tried to imagine a really unlikely spot. There was a smell of rain, and all the plants were drooping. I used the trowel my father had given me. I don't know why I was doing this thing with my money, but it seemed like an excellent idea. And I chose a good, secret place for it all.

Each evening I performed a ritual. I ate some food; two slices of toast and marmite cut into postage stamp pieces. Then I drank a cup of camomile tea. Anything else made me feel deathly ill, and I was afraid to eat it. I thought that if I did all my insides might pour out like a thin emulsion, and I'd be unable to stand up and carry on. After posting squares of toast into my mouth and systematically swallow-ing I arranged myself on the sofa in front of the TV. Just on the off-chance someone looked in through the window. There I'd be, lounging, engrossed in a programme. In fact I sat there like a mannequin. The real me was groping about, banging into things, ripping my hair, shredding my cheeks. Screaming for him to come back.

I had two letters in the post on the same day. Two white envelopes spread out on the mat like the wings of a dead dove. My parents wrote to say they loved me. I found it difficult to decipher the words; my eyes weren't working properly. They said they had to mention the man I was living with. How unhappy they were about that. They'd heard bad things about him. They said it wasn't too late. Why didn't I pack a bag and stay with them? Nobody's angry with you, the letter said. Just come home to us. I wondered what they were talking about; I was home. The other came from the HR department. They regretted to have to inform me that I was required to attend a second warning interview. And could I respond within seven days. And in the meantime not to come into work. This was standard procedure, the letter said.

I had a delayed reaction to the letters. After I'd read them I enjoyed ripping them both up into confetti. Then I sank to the floor and sobbed. So not actually such a huge delay. I cried until I was numb, my head rocking on the confetti-strewn carpet. I didn't have a tissue, and my face stung bitterly. Later I heard steps on the path to my house. Then vigorous banging. I held onto the walls and the hall table as I ran to open the door. He sprang in and lifted me up in his arms. As I ran my fingers through his hair I could hear laughter. You've been crying, he said, and let me down gently. If it's about the car I can explain. The car doesn't matter, I said, now you're here. That's good, he said, 'cos my mate needs it for a couple more days.

He wanted something to eat. He said soup would do. As I prepared it for him he sat at the kitchen table and talked to me. All the time he talked his foot tapped the floor. He

smoked a cigarette. Everything had changed. Even the utensils on the walls stood to attention; I could hear them clang
against each other. He asked me if I had any news. No, I
said, and kissed his forehead. He ate quickly, ripping chunks
of bread apart, and dunking them into his bowl. Then he
picked me up again. What's happening? I asked him, although
I didn't care where he took me. Wait and see, he said, and
ran upstairs with me in his arms. Oh yes, he said, and plonked
me on the bed. He quickly took his clothes off. We've got
time for a sly one, he said, and climbed on top of me. Then
we're off to a party.

I don't like parties

I SEARCHED THROUGH my wardrobe for something to wear. Everything was too dark and corporate. The few special, slinky things seemed too special and, well, slinky. When I asked him what sort of party it was, he said the usual sort, and looked at me as if I was mental. Is someone celebrating something? I said, as I tried to tidy my hair at the mirror. God, I was way beyond plain, almost ugly. My eyes were like currants in raw pastry.

Finally I put on jeans and an unfamiliar, smocky kind of top I found hiding under some shirts. I can't think what had possessed me to buy it. Usually I wouldn't be seen dead in something like that. He wanted to listen to music, have a drink. He said it would get us in the mood. What mood? I asked. And for what? He stood in the bedroom doorway, and pointed at me. OK, he said, what is it with you and all these questions? What are you, some crap private detective? he asked. I know, he said, showing all his teeth in a grin. You're Miss fucking Marple the Second. Holy shit, he laughed, pretend-ing to look at me through binoculars, you actually look a bit like her. Turns me right off anyway. I sat on the bed, and looked at him grinning, filling the door frame. Then he went downstairs. I felt an icy scarf creep round my neck. I don't want to go to a party, I told the mirror and all the things in my bedroom.

By the time we were picked up by one of his friends we were both drunk. The bass from the speakers in the car was strong enough to melt your brain. I sat on his lap, and collapsed on to him. The back seat was already jammed with blokes. For the entire journey he ran his hands over my body, and pushed his swollen cock against me. I looked out at the streets where ordinary people shopped and talked to each other. I sort of wanted to wind down the window, and shout at them to help me. But it did look boring out there. Safe and boring, I thought. Someone in the car was passing a bottle of vodka around. He grabbed it. Drink up, he yelled. You need to zone out a bit. He took a swig, and held it to my lips.

We screeched interminably through a housing estate. When we stopped I couldn't get out of the car; my body was so lax and heavy. We had to fight our way. A crowd of people stood around in the garden smoking and drinking. He carried me through the open door of a house, and laid me on a sofa. Won't be long, he said, and gave me a full, uncorked bottle of red wine.

As soon as he'd gone I began to feel hyper-awake and

excited. I spilled wine down my stupid top as I gulped it. Dim lamps glowed in the lounge, and I could only just make out the shapes of people. The music was so deafening no one was talking. They seemed to be absorbed in touching each other instead. I wasn't sure if anybody could see me, and that made me happy. Eventually I had to get up to find the loo. I didn't want to leave my sofa; it felt like a little boat that magically no one could board.

Bodies were propped on every step of the stairs, drinking and smoking. I picked my way between them. I was unsteady on my feet, but no one seemed to mind if I stepped on them. There was a queue for the loo. The woman in front of me turned, and I realised I'd seen her before. I tapped her shoulder, and as she faced me slowly I knew who she was. She coughed the cough I remembered. How's your dog? I asked her. I told her I was the person who'd given her a note. What note? she said, without the slightest interest. Then she focused on me. Oh yeah, she said, and took a long drag from her cigarette. Are you OK? she asked me through a cloud of smoke, narrowing her eyes. I asked her why I shouldn't be. It seemed like a weird question to ask a stranger. Just wondered, she answered, and went into the loo.

I crept through the house. There were two guys snogging on the bed in what looked like a child's room. I stood and watched them. They seemed really sweet; at least they had each other. One of them noticed me. What's your name? he said, fondling his chest and belly. I told him I didn't remember. That can happen, he smiled, and patted the bed. Are you on your own? Why don't you come and lie down with us? The other guy looked as if he'd dozed off. I said I didn't think I would do that. I was with my partner, and he might not like it if I did. The guy put his head to one side. No problem, babe, he said, and held my hand.

I sat on the edge of the bed, and realised I was totally on my own. The man massaged my fingers. No offence, but I think you need to loosen up a bit, he said softly, you seem really tense. That's not even one bit true, I answered, and stood up. I couldn't be more relaxed and happy. God, I sounded like some head-girly heroine in an Enid Blyton school story. The bedroom felt tiny and airless. OK, OK, the man said, and lay back down. Say hello to your partner for me when he surfaces, won't you?

I negotiated the stairs and made my way to the kitchen. People were gathered round a table with food arranged on it. Even though I wasn't hungry I struggled to get through. Next to a mug of buttercups there were bottles of wine and cans of lager. In the centre I could see a huge bowl filled with tomatoes and foreign-looking lettuce leaves, a pile of bread rolls, and various cheeses arranged on a wooden board. Sausages and burgers were being handed round. People offered me things and I accepted everything. The wine was warm, perhaps at blood temperature. The cheese was crumbly and sharp, then creamy and mild. The flavours of everything tasted extreme.

I looked around at all the chewing people. Frilly lettuce hung out of their mouths. All these human beings, I thought, but he isn't among them. Not one of them was lovely him. I looked but couldn't see his blond curls anywhere. Not one person knew who I was. I spat out the lump of sausage stuck in my mouth, and dropped my plate on the tiled kitchen floor. The room was so noisy it smashed soundlessly. I began to cry, then I was sitting on an easy chair in a quieter room. I fell asleep, and woke up when a girl came round with a huge plate of hash brownies. Everyone cheered. There was coffee, and a liqueur tasting of cough medicine. I had some of that. I knew I had to be careful but the brownies were so tender and moistly chocolatey I ate four.

I go to the pictures

I ENDED UP at the back of the house, and fell over a child's bike as I stumbled about. Finally I found something to sit on. My leg felt wet so I examined it. A street light cast an electric aura into the garden that made the grass and trees look as if they were coated in mauve suede. Warm tar-black blood ran down my leg. The weird thing was it didn't hurt at all, even though the cut looked long and deep. I watched it spread. Everything was dead; rinsed of colour, muffled and still. There was total silence, whilst above me the grey trees gyrated about.

I wasn't sure where I was, or how I'd got here. The house looked as if it might be burning down, but I didn't care. Every smoky window was lit up, and the figures of people writhed around each other. Actually, no. It was a party, I remembered. Those people were having fun whilst I buggered about in the monochrome garden, bleeding as usual. I could see a rabbit hutch behind some bins so I went to have a look. I had to kneel on the stiff, scorched grass. It was surprisingly beautiful inside that little hutch.

Behind the wire mesh of the cage window vivid moving scenes were playing out. I made myself more comfortable, and peered in: tiny elephants crashed through emerald palm trees. The scenes were soundless, but I could tell the elephants were trumpeting, or whatever they do when they're stampeding through a forest. Each elephant had a sparkling jewel on its forehead, and sweet painted feet. Then the elephants became bundles of monkeys darting through ruined palaces at unbelievable speeds. In the second window dancing girls in purple saris whirled around, their miniature hands atwitch, their black lips like strange new moons.

As I watched the pictures changed. Ravishing, naked people with perfect, glistening bodies were torturing captives. Blood and entrails wormed their way through the rabbit hutch straw. Things were being done to the pinkest, most perfect-looking babies. I could hear faint screams, and from the little babies the most heart-wrenching sounds. I was unable to unhook my fingers from the wires of the cage. I had to stay and watch, even though I was shuddering with horror. Then the scenes faded, and I got up. Before I left I bent down to have a final look. Two huge, benign-looking rabbits were sleeping inside.

I ran out of the garden, and saw my car. It had a broken mirror, and a dent in the driver's door, but it was mine. I felt the bonnet; it was warm, as if there were a big, living heart beating inside. The driver's door was ajar, and the keys were in the ignition, so I climbed in. I loved it inside my car. I decided to go home. I kept checking the speedometer; I wanted to stay around thirty. I was trembling, and icy with sweat. I caught sight of my face in the rear-view mirror, stretched into an immobile grin, and almost crashed. Maybe that wasn't me, I thought. Maybe a maniac was in the back of my car.

I parked in front of my house. It was a miracle, but there I was. The sky was lightening, but all I yearned to do was get inside, lock the doors, close the curtains, and snuggle down into my bed. I was incapable of lifting my head from the steering wheel. I thought I could hear a siren continuously sounding. There was someone banging on the car window. One of my do-gooder neighbours was gesticulating to me through the glass, only I couldn't hear a thing with the mad siren wailing away. He was getting redder and redder so I straightened up, and wound the window down. Immediately the siren stopped, and I realised it had been the car horn, activated by my stupid head on the wheel. I climbed out, and pushed past him. I couldn't tell what he was clucking about.

My parents were in the kitchen, wearing their fleeces, drinking tea at my table. Mum had done some cooking. Before you ask, my father said, we got your spare key from Alison. We came round last night but you weren't here so we tidied round a bit for you, my mum told me, and tried to hold my hand. Want a nice cuppa? Your father brought his mower, didn't you, Daddy? He spruced up your lawn. My father took a sip of tea. I stood in the doorway. We came back this morning. We were so worried about you. Well, honestly, she said eventually. The very least you could do is say thank you.

I began to laugh again. I didn't want to but it was as if the sound emerged from my mouth in an endless squawking hiccup. I think anyone would have done the same; the look on my parents' faces was enough to make a depressed gibbon guffaw. I could see my poor mother staring at the wound on my leg. I knew she was dying to get at it with Savlon and plasters. I doubled over, and slid down the edge of the door. Get out, both of you, I screamed. I hope you drop dead. Get out of my life and never come back.

I plan my menus

I WATCHED A lot of TV, there was nothing else to do. He liked me to be available, so I didn't go out much. And I found it freeing, somehow, to know my aged p's weren't going to pop up at inconvenient times any more. It gave me more space, more scope. Things seemed simpler. Even so, one day, after about a week of not seeing them, I stood still in the bedroom, and felt my heart flip and right itself as I realised how much I loved the silly old things. I was stricken by knowing it, seared by the picture of them patiently waiting in the kitchen. Pottering around; mowing and baking, trying to be helpful. I nearly broke down and blubbed when I thought how upset and sad they would be about the way things had turned out. But it was no good going there. I had stumbled through some sort of security door that could never be opened from my side. So I briskly made the bed and opened the window. The curtains rippled on a breeze smelling of freshly cut grass, and I felt ready for action.

At the supermarket it was blessed business as usual. Was I a tiny bit unhinged, loving the supermarket? I always found it spiritually uplifting, drifting round amongst the orderly racks and labyrinthine aisles. I loved lobbing nice things into my trolley. Anything you wanted there was a huge sign, guiding you. Today they had Hammond organ arrangements of middle of the road pop songs surging through the store. It was the final, perfect touch. I bought the ingredients to make a chicken curry, and had fun choosing the accompaniments before getting engrossed in the stuff for a beef casserole, then spent some time in the wines and spirits section; I thought I'd better stock up on booze. I tried not to speculate about where he was, or what he had been doing at the party without me.

I was nervous I might bump into my parents. There's nothing they like better than a good shopping expedition. At every bend I expected to see them, maybe in their Pacamacs, string bags at the ready, peering at the ingredients of something they would never dream of eating, their bifocals at that particular angle needed in order to see. But no, they weren't shopping today. I felt disappointed, bereft almost. If they had been there I'd have hidden from them, of course.

In the café I wasn't sure what to eat; there were so many choices. But also I wasn't hungry. The idea of eating seemed far-fetched. When I tried to recall when I had last eaten I was shocked. Nothing came to mind. I knew I'd spat out a sausage in a crowded kitchen. Then I remembered eating cheese and a bread roll, how delicious they'd tasted. Maybe I was still digesting those brownies. I knew I'd eaten after that, otherwise I would be dead by now. Weirdly I could almost hear Alison telling me to eat, so I settled on a baked potato and some apple juice. When the meal came the potato was crowned with a jagged head of chilled, pale yellow, quasi-cheese fragments. It was as if an alien had tried to simulate a tasty earthling snack. I pushed the bits off, and nibbled forkfuls of cool spud, watching the queue for the café till.

The back of one of the waiting women was familiar. She was surrounded by a milling team of children. A boy of about twelve was touching the doughnuts and licking his hands. Some of the very small ones were actually swinging off her coat. She ignored them all. Finally, as I watched, she seemed to switch on and notice something. With a surprising economy of movement she slapped the twelve-year-old across the side of his head, and pushed the little ones aside. Then she coughed that familiar cough, and I knew she was the woman from the party loo, the same woman I had seen at the scratched door when I tried to find his house. I felt as if I'd been electrocuted. Why was I bumping into this woman? Was I following her without knowing? Or was she following me?

I hid behind my menu, riveted by the woman and her children. I remembered the way she'd taken the note I handed her. How she'd said she couldn't promise anything. Her total lack of interest. And then, at the party, how she'd asked me if I was OK. The boy she'd struck was sitting at a separate table from the main group, sulking and wiping his eyes. I could see he'd been crying. They all looked dishevelled and not very clean, but his trousers were halfway up his legs and his trainers had no laces.

Then I realised; he was the boy who'd been sat in my lounge, on my sofa, watching football on my TV. The boy with the whispery voice. My scalp began to twitch and stretch; I thought how twilight zoney it all was. Maybe the universe was checking me out. Even trying to warn me, or something. The other children were bolting down bowls of chips with what looked like gravy on top. He wasn't getting any. I could almost have felt sorry for him, if I hadn't been so freaked out. Wait, I told myself, calm down; perhaps I was having one of those days when everybody seems familiar. I looked at the other people in the café. No, I didn't recognise anybody. But still, it couldn't be the universe or whatever. The universe didn't give a shit about me. Nobody did. I was terrified though. It was like being in a film where you don't know you're being stalked, but the audience does.

I don't know how I got out of the café. I slung the groceries into the boot of the car, and sat behind the wheel. I couldn't think straight. My mind was as smooth and flat as the baize of a billiard table; the things I needed to think about kept sliding away like gently nudged billiard balls. What was I doing? Did I imagine a beef casserole would reorder my life? I don't know how long I sat in the car park before finally deciding to go home and wait for him. Then we could talk things through, come to some understanding. If I didn't like what he had to say I would finish with him. All this stuff was a sign. I had to sort my life out. It was that simple.

I cook up a storm

FOR TWO WEEKS I thought about how I was going to tell
him. I carried on doing things. He was in my house with
me. Then he would go out. The days were like a series of
black and white snap shots. In, out, black, white. Sometimes
I went to town, but I didn't buy anything. I felt mesmerised
by my own life. On the day I'd got home from the supermarket I'd tipped all the food into the freezer. A few times I
remembered the chunks of beef and chicken, waiting in the
frozen dark for me to do something with them. At last I
realised at least I could do some cooking. That would be a
start. Finally I got them out of the freezer.

The next afternoon I was alone. I'd been alone for three
days. His phone was off, he didn't call. I had a couple of
glasses of red wine, then embarked on making my casserole.
The spirit of Delia hovered over me in the kitchen. Yes, yes,
she soothed, mmmm, yes. And may I just say what an amazing, shit-hot cook you are? She even commented on the way

I browned the meat in small batches. Oh Delia, I told her, of course. We don't want them to frigging steam, after all. This is all about caramelisation. La la, and thrice la, she sang, swooping and banking up by the fluorescent light strip. It verily is. And no, dear, we frigging do not. Then I heard someone at the front door, so I opened the window wide for her to fly out before I answered it.

In the hallway I felt my heart thumping in my throat. Through the frosted glass panel loomed the shape of a man. I knew it couldn't be him; he never knocked. But my legs wouldn't move, so I had to lean forward, and hope they'd catch up with my body. Somehow I plodded to the door and opened it. A goofy-looking youth wanted to read the meter. I cannot say if I hugged him. I hope not, but can't say definitely that I didn't. I did insist he show me some ID; anything to keep him from leaving quickly. Unfortunately he didn't look as if he'd be much use in a crisis; far too weedy and trembly.

Are you new at this? I asked him. He was fumbling for ages in his little shoulder bag. Only you seem a bit scared. It's not as if you've got to construct the thing, you know. Just read the numbers. Excuse me, please, he said, and pushed past. Show me where your meter is, if you wouldn't mind. Oh dear, I'm sorry, I said, following him along the hall. Have I hurt your feelings? No, madam, you have not, he told me. In comparison to some houses I visit you are quite polite. And whatever you've got in that oven smells good. I could have cried, it seemed such a nice thing to say. I didn't know you worked on a Saturday, I called after him as he walked away, but he didn't respond. Why should he? It was a stupid comment to make.

After he left I went into the garden. The grass was looking neat, and I noticed a row of begonias my dad must have planted when they came round. The patio chairs had patches of rust on them. I sat down. Out here the sun winked into the small puddles. Under the laurel bushes, in its strong little box, nestled my lovely stash of money. In the oven the casserole gently bubbled. Birds hopped on the table and looked sideways at me, then flew away. I could hear their wings whirr. A breeze rhythmically lifted my hair, and dropped it back against my face. I began to feel I was the only human being left in the world. Empty houses, silent streets, abandoned cars, childless schools, all stretched out from my garden in every direction.

I was already completely over the idea of the casserole, but I checked it anyway, and peeled potatoes. I laid the table, and put out some candles. It was almost evening when he came back. He seemed subdued. Something smells good, he said. I gave him a glass of wine, and he sprawled on a chair in the kitchen. I asked him if he was okay. He said he had the bitch of all hangovers. He drank his wine quickly, and poured another. Hair of the mangy dog, he said, and raised his glass. I strained the potatoes, and added butter and warm milk to them. He asked me what I was doing. I'm making creamed spuds, I said. He told me he didn't know how you did that, so I showed him. He stood beside me, and listened as I explained. Then I gave him a taste. Shit, he said, that's amazing.

I lit the candles, and opened another bottle of wine. Everything was peaceful. We sat together in the warm kitchen eating the casserole and potatoes. He had seconds. I looked at him as he sat drinking his wine. He was beautiful; his broad shoulders, his strong, brown neck. The perfect shape of his lips. Your hair is getting long, I said, and got up to stand behind him. I asked if I could comb it for him. If you like, he said sleepily. As I combed his blond curls I tried to frame the questions I'd rehearsed. It was impossible. He dropped his head back onto my chest, and I bent and kissed his forehead.

He said he felt like chilling on the sofa. I went to the bathroom, and locked the door. I looked at myself in the mirror above the sink, and slapped my laughably rosy cheeks. What was I doing? A person couldn't just come and go like this. Couldn't invade someone's life without an invitation. Abandon someone at a party. Gatecrash a family funeral. I sat on the loo, and rubbed my eyes until all I could see were crimson blobs. I thought about other things he'd done to me. Things I had let him do. They weren't good things. He wasn't good for me.

Apart from the fact that I probably had some sort of gross STI, all my friends had gone, and my parents were sobbing, their blood pressure zooming out of control at this very moment because I had been so horrible to them. The thought of him spread out on the sofa made my forehead prickle and itch. I wanted to rush about, and collect all the crap belongings he always dropped here and there, and throw them to hell. His underwear entwined with mine in the washing basket made me heave. I couldn't have him in my house any more. Everything became brilliantly shiny and smooth, like the surface of a pool as it recovers from a stone's throw. I had to get rid of him. It wasn't too late to put my life back on some sort of track, even salvage my job if I tried hard enough.

I crept downstairs, impatient to get it over with. I shook him until he stirred. Finally he awoke. What the fuck is going on? he said. What's happened? He stood up, and looked quickly around. Then he squinted his eyes at me. Have you flipped? he said. You'd better have a good reason for waking me up. I heard my voice saying I wanted him out of my house, out of my life. I told him I didn't even like him. My voice piped away like a mechanical bird's. Get out now, I shrilled. And never come back. You don't love me, you don't even know me. He started to laugh. I beat his chest with my fists. He thought it was funny. So I slapped his face.

His expression changed immediately. His mouth grew ugly. With stiff fingers he patted my cheek firmly three times, not very hard, but I lost my balance and fell over, hitting my head on the coffee table. No one had ever done anything like that to me before. He might as well have smashed in my skull with a baseball bat. I knew the blood in my veins and arteries was stalling. I could sense things coagulate as I lay on the carpet. I felt so stupid.

We'll pretend this hasn't happened, he said, stretching his arms above his head and yawning. Then he bent over, and inspected me as I lay on the floor. You're going to tick me off once too often, he said in a confidential way, and helped me up, straightening my clothes. Then we'll all be very sorry. I swayed a little as he lay down on the sofa again, adjusting the pillows behind his head. Bummer really, he said, grunting as he got comfortable. We were having such a great time. Now get lost for a bit. I feel like watching the telly.

I'm on the outside

I WANDERED THROUGH the streets in my neighbourhood. All these pretty gardens, window boxes, trellises. It was amazing how people worked so hard to make their little patches of mud nice. I wondered why they did that. We were all perched on the earth's crust so lightly. Anything could blow us away. The perfumed flowers spilling over garden walls seemed so pitiful to me. The carefully staked ornamental trees made me want to cry, they were so pathetic. We are all skeletons, I thought. Dragging our clicking bones around, clacking about, waiting to collapse and be carted to the rubbish heap. All we can do is grin, grin, grin. Through the lighted windows I passed families gathered together, but they couldn't see me, drifting like a wraith up and down the darkening streets.

My mobile had died. I walked until I found a phone box that wasn't smashed up and pissed in. I left a message for Alison saying I was sorry for everything. That I needed her.

I asked her if she would meet me soon, so I could explain. Lastly I told her I missed her, and I loved her a lot. Standing in the phone box I felt like someone who's been given one last phone call before they disappear into the underworld. Then I went back to the house.

The TV was still chuntering away, and he was asleep on the sofa, so I climbed the stairs and got ready for bed. Before I turned off the bedside light I plugged my phone into the charger, and hid it under the valance. I fell asleep immediately. I woke up to the sound of someone moving about in the room. It was still night time. He was standing at the foot of the bed holding my mobile. You've got a message, he said, and threw the phone towards me. From that interfering cow, Alison. I thought you'd given her the push. I sat up and grabbed my phone. She's not welcome in this house, he said, walking out of the room. But she's my best friend, I called after him, sounding like a primary school kid in the playground. Then I whispered under the covers, This is my house, she can come if I want her to.

In the morning I left him in bed. Before I tiptoed out of the room I watched him sleeping. His face was perfectly serene, and he didn't make the slightest sound as he slept. The scar on his chest was silvery now. It could almost have been the place where someone had extracted his heart, and roughly sewn him back together. Then he sighed, and turned over onto his stomach. He'd come to bed with his shorts on and they rucked up as he turned, exposing one buttock. It looked like some exotic, furry fruit but I had no desire to bite it. I quickly sneaked around getting ready, and went out without even having a glass of water. As I walked away from the house I felt light-headed and alert.

Alison and I had brunch at our fave café in town. We talked about her kids, their teachers and Tom. She told me I wasn't missing anything in work. We ate scrambled eggs and smoked salmon, and sipped orange juice. Alison said it was her treat. She told me they were decorating the kitchen. I watched her lovely face as she spoke, and concentrated on how she formed and projected every word. I felt that if I listened hard and long enough I could piece together some sort of raft that would float me back to the quiet world of decorating and the school run, and even, eventually, stumble on my old self. The food was delicious; I could feel it doing me good. We agreed to keep in touch. She didn't ask me questions, or give me an opinion about my life. I didn't tell her anything. We kissed each other goodbye.

When I got back and opened the front door I could tell there were people around. The TV volume was high, and something was going on in the lounge. I pushed the door open. The room seemed to be full of children. The boy from the café was sprawled on the sofa, and wedged beside him were two toddlers, one asleep, the other sucking from a bottle of baby milk. They looked about two and three. A pair of girls, six and eight maybe, lay on their tummies on the rug watching TV. The room smelled of grubby clothes and unwashed hair. Not one of them took the slightest notice of me. I shut the door and stood in the hallway. For a moment I even thought I'd come into the wrong house.

He was in the kitchen, frying bacon. What's going on? I asked. Making bacon sandwiches, he said, slinging a tea towel over his shoulder. Want one? I sank down on a chair. In my back garden I could see some beaten-up kids' toys and a bike. I felt all my strength slipping out from my extremities. Who are these children? I managed to mouth. What are they doing in my house? He turned, and leaned back on the cooker, grinning. They're mine, he said, folding his arms. What's the big deal? It's only for a couple of hours. But I didn't know you had a family, I said. He pulled me up, and hugged me. Well, you do now, he said. I'll reward you later for being a good girl. Then he kissed me firmly on the mouth.

I have a houseful

I DIDN'T HAVE anywhere to go. I was in my own place, and I didn't know what to do. There was no point in going out into the empty streets. But it felt wrong to be at home. My house was infested with strangers. He was bashing around in the kitchen, his children filled the lounge. I stood in the hallway, and waited. Every so often a child would come out, and go upstairs to the bathroom. Each one ignored me. I looked at myself in the hall mirror. Sure enough there I was, standing in the hall. I watched as my face formed itself into the face of a woman crying, but no tears came out of my eyes. My down-turned mouth looked ridiculous.

There was a shout from the kitchen, and all the children ran out of the lounge cheering and pushing each other. Grub's up, I heard him say. I hovered in the kitchen doorway. The kids sat around silently, eating their bacon and bread with deep intent. What can I give them to drink? he asked. I pointed to the fruit juice. Not sure they'll like that, he said.

I left them, and went into the lounge. The toddlers were both tumbled on the sofa, asleep. I sat on the edge of a chair, and inspected them. Both blond, with pale, luxuriant lashes. Maybe a boy and a girl, I thought.

I talked myself down as I listened to the sleeping babies breathe. I told myself this was OK. I mean, what could be nicer? My lover introduces me to his children. Why so tragic? Why so disturbed? I decided to behave as if this was all normal, nice even. That's what this was. Something I could laugh about with work friends at the water cooler-type stuff. Another part of me was unimpressed. She pointed out some things like, firstly, what friends? Secondly, which water cooler? To be strictly accurate we didn't have one in our office. And also, excuse me, but, *lover*? Who he? She didn't know what he felt for me, but it certainly wasn't lurve. I knew all this was true. I touched one of the babies on its warm leg. I told myself the children weren't to blame. But I blamed them anyway. I actually called them little bastards, to myself. How sad was that?

As I climbed the stairs I heard someone in my bedroom. I felt reluctant to find out who it was, but someone behaving naturally would dash in and find out, so I did. The whispery twelve-year-old was looking through my things. What do you think you're doing? I asked. He was holding something silky, a camisole I think, rubbing it between his hands. Nothing, he said, in his weird little voice. Give that to me, I said. Now. He scrunched it up in his hand, and shoved it in his pocket. What you going to do about it? he said. Tell my dad? and walked slowly past me down the stairs.

I closed the drawers and straightened things out, then lay down under the covers. Though I was rigid and cold I fell asleep quickly. When I woke I got up immediately, and combed my hair. In the bathroom the floor was wet and the loo roll used up. I cleaned up and went downstairs again. He was talking to a woman in the kitchen. I almost didn't care who she was. They were both smoking, and drinking coffee at the table. When she saw me she coughed. I knew it was the woman I'd seen before.

He unfolded himself from the table. Here she is, he said, holding out his hand to me. Sit down. I thought maybe they'd been talking about me, and she was angry, but she seemed completely calm. He started massaging her shoulders, staring at me. He was waiting for something to happen. She tried to shrug him off. I was surprised he didn't react. Instead he went on squeezing her shoulders; I could see it was hurting her. Any questions? he asked me, smiling smugly. He told her I was the mother of all questioners. Never stops, he said, laughing. Why? Where? How? over and over and over. Well, here's my question, she said. Why don't you get lost? He stretched. You two've probably got a lot to talk about, he said. She didn't answer. She just waited for him to leave. He looked from her to me and back several times. Finally he left.

What a wanker, she said. He was hoping for a scene. You know, two women fighting over him. Sort of thing he loves.

She lit a cigarette. OK, what do you want to know? She rested back against the chair. Ask me anything. She was unbelievably thin and white. Like someone who'd spent her lifetime in an underground cavern.

As she took deep drags from her cigarette I asked her if she was his wife. God, no, she laughed quietly and chestily. No one in their right mind would marry that nasty piece of work. So do you live with him then? I felt I had to ask, even though I was indifferent. Are these your children? She leaned across the table and put her hand on mine. She seemed nice, unthreatening; entirely colourless. Even her eyes were pale, like solidified water. Look, she said, yes, I live with him, on and off. Or should I say, he lives with me sometimes, as in, when the mood takes him. Obviously not at the moment of course. And yes, some of these children are his. What I want to know is, how somebody like you got mixed up with him?

I couldn't answer her. The events of the past months were like tears in a pool of water. He sort of swept me up, I suppose, I said. Do you know what I mean? God yes, she said. He is a bloody champion sweeper. But you know that already, don't you? Look, she said, sitting up straight, I know he's gorgeous to look at. Not bad on the shagging front either. So what? He's still an absolute shit. She stubbed out her fag. It's none of my business, but I will tell you this: you're not the first. I've lost count. Then the kids started trooping in. Right, you lot, bugger off outside, she shouted. Wait in the front garden.

She got up as if her joints were stiff, and put her hand on my shoulder. No offence, she said, but my advice to you is, get rid of him ASAP. She shook me gently with her fragile hand. Or he'll suck you dry. She gestured with her thumb towards her concave chest. Just look at me, for God's sake. We gazed at each other. Have you still got a job? I nodded. Not for long though, if you don't do something soon. Am I right? I nodded again.

Thank you, I said as she was leaving. I wanted her to stay with me. She reappeared in the doorway, holding a sleeping child like a sack of washing under each arm. Good luck, she said. You'll need it. He can be such a charmer when he wants something. She gestured around. And this is all very comfortable for him, I can see. She gave me a little smile. I know, I don't practise what I preach. And let me guess, you've fallen out with your friends? Make it up with them. You'll need all the friends you can get.

The house was quiet and I sat down to absorb it. Then I started to clear up. There was a lot to do, but I did it, dragging myself around. It felt important to get the house neat and sorted, so I didn't stop till it was done. I threw open the back door and the windows, but the smell of smoke and bacon lingered. Also the smell of stale clothes and grubby kids permeated the lounge so I lit a perfumed candle in there. Then whisked up a chicken curry with all the trimmings, opened a bottle of wine and started drinking.

When he came back he plonked himself on the sofa, turned

the TV on and opened the first of a six pack of lager he'd
bought. I served him the food on a tray. I was weaving about
but he didn't seem to mind. He wasn't very interested in
eating, but he drank several cans of lager. He messed the cooling curry with his fork and continued to smoke, watching
the TV. I stood over him with my wine glass in my hand.
Why didn't you tell me you were involved with someone? I
said, gesturing so that wine spilled on the coffee table. Bloody
oops, I said. And how many more kids have you got? How
many more women? He went on drinking, his face dark red.
Answer me, I sobbed, kicking his foot with mine.

He shouted for me to move away from the telly, so I stood
in front of it. He said he was only going to tell me one more
time. The TV remote was in his lap so I snatched it, and
started flicking through the channels. I wanted something to
happen, and this seemed like a good beginning. He looked
funny, trying to catch me as I danced around, but I didn't
laugh. I could hear myself crying. He lost his balance and fell
back into the chair. As I watched him breathing heavily I
became afraid. He was sweating, his hands bunched into fists.
Suddenly I couldn't remember what we were fighting about.
I felt as if someone had emptied me out, like the contents of
an untidy bag.

I get blue

HE LEAPED UP, and knocked the candle over. Hot wax splashed across the coffee table. I'm so sorry, I said, putting it back on its holder. I'm drunk, I don't know what I'm doing. He was breathing heavily. You'd better get out of my way, he said, pushing past me. Seriously, you're very lucky I haven't given you a good smack. He went to the kitchen, and dropped his uneaten curry into the washing-up water. I followed him. Curry sauce was splattered all over the dishes in the sink, bleeding into the water. Pieces of chicken bobbed around. For Christ's sake, he said, squeezing my shoulder hard, stop following me. What are you, my fucking pet?

I tried to put my arms round him. I didn't like him being angry with me. Get out of my fucking way before I do something you'll regret, he shouted. What's wrong with your curry? I said. Shall I make you something else? A bowl of soup? A sandwich? I wanted to be quiet, but I couldn't. Some other girl was staggering through the house, apologising, trying to embrace him. He put his face close to mine again. It was a thing he liked doing, getting in people's faces. Piss off, can't you? he said slowly, punctuating each word with a violent jab to my chest. Each jab drove me back until I was against the wall. Then he stomped upstairs.

I sat on the edge of the sofa, and looked at my untouched plate. I thought perhaps I should eat the naan bread, but I didn't pick it up. My shoulder was aching. I felt the shape of his hand there. *Coronation Street* had just started. I could smell the extinguished candle. I listened hard for any sound from upstairs. The spots where he'd poked me were like deep, burning holes. I heard him flush the toilet, and walk to the bedroom. Then what sounded like drawers opening and closing. The wardrobe door creaked. Then thudding. I felt the strain of listening centre itself in the base of my neck.

The time was 7.43 p.m. when he opened the front door and slammed it behind him. I ran up to the bedroom. My clothes were slung over the bed and drooping out of drawers. He'd been looking for money. And then he'd left. No one else was with me. I knew that. No other imaginary girl was here, sobbing in another room. I lay on the bed, and gathered up the shirt he had thrown down. I sniffed the underarms. The bedroom was cold. I made a comfortable place in the pillow, and tried to shut my eyes. Each time they closed, something would yank them open again. Finally, though, I fell asleep.

When I woke the street lights were shining in. The room was striped and gloomy. I lay shivering, and remembered my dream. I had been in a cave strewn with straw. I was lying in the arms of a fully-grown lioness. She was purring, her face close to mine. Her breath smelled of old meat. I looked at her sleeping eyelids, her eyelashes. Her breaths were deep and long-drawn. We were warm and relaxed lying there together. Her back leg was over me, the paw resting behind my bent knees. I had my arms round her furry neck. Then slowly I realised the danger I was in. I slipped my arms free, and lifted her back leg off. I tried to inch out from underneath her. She reared up, and bared her teeth; her yellow eyes at once wide open. We looked at each other. Then I woke. I recalled staring out from behind the lioness's eyes into my own face. I sat up. The house was silent. I remembered I was on my own.

In the bathroom I sat on the loo seat, and rested my head on the sink. The tap dripped. In the bath there was a spider, and some blond pubic hairs. I reached down and picked them up. The spider raced for the plughole. I don't want you, I said. I opened the bathroom window, and let the hairs fly out into the night. The room filled with rain-laden air. I could hear cars swishing past. I wondered where he could be. Who he was with.

I looked at my reflection in the mirror, and pulled down the neck of my jumper. A dark love bite showed on my neck. And, further down, the shape of his hand. I turned on the shower, and took my clothes off. Four fat, blue bruises like pansies bloomed, two near my collarbone, two on my right breast. My skin sprang into goose bumps. I turned the water to hot, and let the flow drum onto my shoulders. It was easy to cry in the downpour, but I didn't. My back burned, but still I stood. Then I washed myself clean. I stepped out into the cold air, and put his towelling robe on. I took a box from the cabinet, and opened it. I sat on the toilet, and read the instructions. Then I peed on the stick. Urine gushed warmly onto my fingers. There it was. I watched as a perfect, bright, summer-blue line formed.

I go head over heels

THEN I WAS alone. I was alone for maybe three days, or four. About four, I think. During that time I sat at the bottom of the stairs, and dozed. I wasn't really alone, in a way. I had the tiny comma inside me that was a baby, though I didn't feel able to think about it much. Now and then I got up, and drifted round the house. In the kitchen the curry in the sink congealed. I nibbled on the hardened naan bread I'd left by the side of the sofa. I didn't turn the TV off. I pretended this was an everyday sort of house.

I dragged down the duvet from my bed, and made a sleeping area at the foot of the stairs. I needed to stay by the front door. I had chocolate in my bag, and I rationed it out. I drank plenty of water. At eight thirty every morning the postman came. Each time I thought it was him, coming back to me. I had one letter, from the office. It said they were regretfully terminating my employment. I decided I'd think about that later.

I showered when I saw the sky getting light, and washed my hair. I let it dry naturally. My curls came back, and I didn't stop them. I put on perfume. I changed my night-gown. Then there was an evening when he turned up and brought some friends with him. He ignored me sitting at the bottom of the stairs. They all walked into the lounge. One of the women went to the kitchen. I could hear her clearing up. They put on music. It sounded like a party.

I thought I should show myself so I went into the lounge. The two women were dancing close together, feeling each other. They were drinking from bottles, swigging lazily. One was laughing, and pushing her leg up into the crotch of the other. He was lying on the sofa, smoking something that created a thick smell, watching the women with his eyes half closed. He wasn't wearing a shirt. His feet were bare. I wondered if I was dreaming perhaps. No one seemed to notice me. I sat in a chair, and wrapped the duvet around me. With his free hand he rubbed his groin slowly.

Even inside the duvet I was cold. I felt I should go to bed. He got up, and they were all dancing together. The women were naked from the waist up. He was squeezing the blond woman's breasts, making the other woman suck her nipples. I got up, and dragged the duvet round me. I stood in the doorway. He pulled off the blond woman's skirt, she seemed drunk, floppy. Underneath she was naked. He bent her over the back of the easy chair. He and the other woman started stroking her buttocks. He eased her legs far apart.

They started running their fingers up and down the flesh between her buttocks where it was darker, like a bruise. They slapped her in turn, each time harder. She drooped over the chair back, and lay with her head in the seat cushion, her arms hanging forward. I heard her groan. I watched from the doorway. It looked as if she was asleep. He was holding an empty beer bottle. He gave it to the dark woman. She worked the bottle into the sleeping woman's anus with both her hands, wiggling it slightly from side to side. She held it against herself, as if it were a penis. He was laughing. I saw the shining bottle inch into her. It stretched her as it went in. She didn't seem to notice. I heard a tinkling sound. The sleeping woman was urinating down the back of my chair. They left her there with the bottle gaping out of her.

Up in the bedroom the music sounded like a heartbeat, strangely comforting. I lay down on the bed. I couldn't stop shivering. My jaw was rigid, my teeth vibrated against each other. Then I felt myself drifting away, each pulse of the music pushing me further into a dark, safe place.

I woke up the instant the light was snapped on. Both the women were there. They seemed drunk and happy. He threw back the covers, and pulled me down the bed by my ankles. I screamed as I fell onto the floor. He shouted something I couldn't understand into my face. I held onto his leg. I asked him to let me stay. He kicked me off. I crawled to the landing. He followed me. The woman was calling him, laughing throatily. I kneeled at his feet. Please let me stay, I said. I kissed his foot. Now you've made me really mad, he said quietly. This is your own entire fucking fault. Then he kicked me with all his strength. I was like a sack of old shoes falling down the stairs. I thought about my tiny baby. I pictured her minuscule arm buds flapping, her rudimentary lips sounding, ouch, ouch, ouch. I hoped she was cushioned safely, deep inside.

I bleed publicly

ALISON SAID I ought to eat. She went up to the counter, and ordered poached eggs. We were at a window booth. I took off my wet coat, and rubbed my damp shoulders. My face itched as it dried. Outside the rain fell in a Monday morning way, straight and never-ending. I watched the street. Nothing was happening. In the café they were playing pan pipe versions of songs from *The Sound of Music*. Alison came back to the table. You've got to laugh, she said. I mean, pan pipes. She sat, and undid her mac. Well, don't hate me, I said, but I actually quite like the sound of pan-pipes. We sang along to 'How Do You Solve a Problem Like Maria?' Appropriate, I said. Alison didn't smile. Now this one I really love, I said, 'Edelweiss'. I'm shocked, she said. I never had you down as an 'Edelweiss' person.

There was a pause while she took her coat half off. Alison, you don't know me at all, I said. Come to think of it, I don't know myself any more. I'm pregnant, I said, and I spelled it out: P–R–E–G–G–E–R–S. Then, because she looked so blank, I said, With sprog, knocked up? You know, bunny in the oveny? I tried to hum 'I Whistle a Happy Tune'. I could see Alison didn't recognise it.

OK, she said. That's it. I'm going to tell your parents. They should know what's what. I got up to go. If you do that I will never speak to you again, I said. I will never forgive you. Promise me you won't. But why? she asked. Why not let them care for you? They love you. I told her I knew they did. It's complicated, I said. All this shit is something I need to sort out myself for once. Or I'll never grow up. Say you understand? Well, yes, I can see that, she said slowly, and looked at me seriously. Say it, I said. Yes, I promise, she said. But only for the time being. And I'm getting you a doctor's appointment. That's not open to negotiation. I sat back down. I got into this, I told her, I know I can get out of it. Kindly, she said nothing.

A waitress brought my eggs. I stabbed each trembling egg yolk, and watched as the yellows poured out. Funny, isn't it? I asked her. We always seem to eat eggs when we meet. She didn't answer. She hadn't said anything for a while. You should eat something, she finally said. Go on, please try to eat a few mouthfuls. Her eyes were blurry with tears. She asked if I needed money as she watched me put a bendy piece of egg white on my fork. Before it reached my mouth it slithered off. Saved, I said. More coffee then? she suggested, and got up. I'll ask them to make it with milk. She looked at my shaking hands, and bit her lip. Won't be long, she said, and went back to the counter.

I watched her bustling up to the counter. She felt to me like someone I'd known in another dimension. Someone I had loved. When she came back with two mugs of coffee she said it was time I told her what was happening. She busied herself sugaring my drink and stirring it. Drink up first. I opened my mouth. I really wanted to spill the whole story, but somehow I didn't have enough words. On one level it was all so piti-fully predictable. If I laid it all out in front of Alison she would, with her clear blue eyes, evaporate it, sort it so easily that I'd never forgive her. Maybe I wanted to see it as a bit tragic and hugely unique, even though I knew really it wasn't. Eventually I said, thanks for the offer of moolah, anyway. Money is not the problem.

I told her I had a headache. She found some tablets in her bag. Are these OK for you to have now? she asked, holding the pack away from me. For God's sake, I said, just hand the stupid things over. After being kicked down the stairs two little tablets are not going to matter. I could probably take the whole box. I'm invincible. Don't talk like that, she said. My brain was heavy. I felt my forehead was going to fall out. I rested my head in my hands. My God, Alison said, and leaned across to feel my head. Is that what he's done? Her hand was cool. In the same instant that she touched my skin startlingly bright blood gushed from my nose, and plopped like flat coins onto my plate of messed-up eggs.

I can't stop myself

IT GAVE ME time to think, that quiet week being alone in my house. I asked myself why I should care about being alone. It was what I wanted, after all. Perhaps he'd left for good. I made a few plans. Very simple ones. Then he came back, and I had to rethink them. I found it difficult; it was as if the section of my brain that knew about good moves for me was talking at cross purposes with the section of my heart that knew about him. Somehow I got things straight.

He behaved as if nothing had happened. Mostly he slept and watched TV. I phoned Alison. Have you got company? Alison asked. I told her I wanted to see her. We agreed to meet soon. Just before she rang off I told her I had a plan. Are you leaving him? she asked. Well, one of us is leaving, put it that way, I said. She asked me what that meant. Wait and see, I said.

I sat down beside him on the settee. He put his arm round my shoulders and began to kiss me. I opened my mouth without thinking. Stand up, he said. Take off your blouse. As I undid the buttons I asked if I should turn off the TV. No, he said, I'm waiting for the football. He told me to take off my trousers. As I undid the zip I felt myself splitting. Part of me drifted up, and hovered over the TV. The other part centred down between my legs. I felt myself beginning to warmly liquefy there.

I moved near him, and pressed my belly towards his mouth. Kiss me, I said. Say you love me. It felt very important that he tell me. Say I love you, I asked him again. No, he said. He pushed my bra up over my breasts, and pressed his index fingers down into the soft centres. How do you feel now? he said. What do you want? Do I make you sick? Tell me. He grabbed the waistband of my knickers, and bunched it up in his hand, pulling it upwards. I toppled nearer to him. Does it hurt you? he asked. I felt the bite of the material as it thinned and tightened, I felt a dull pulse in my anus. Do you like it? he said. Yes, I said, I do. You can't do without me, can you, poor baby? he said. You need me. I think I'll come back for good. You know, and never, ever leave. I know that's what you really want.

Without letting go he undid his trousers, and let them fall. I pulled his prick free. I wanted to bite it hard. No you don't, he said. He pushed me, and I lay back on the settee. Do it now, I said into his blond hair. He manoeuvred the taut material to one side, and forced his penis in through the narrow gap. It hurts, he said, and pulled harder. As we came he said, Look at me, watch me. But I clutched his hair and stared at my other self, my floating self. I thought, She must pity me. She reminded me of my plan just by floating there.

I dig without due care

I LAY AWAKE the following morning. When it was six o'clock it was time to get out of bed. I wanted to do it without disturbing him. He lay on his back, his leg resting across my thighs. I began to push him off. He muttered, then turned to lie on his side facing me. He flung his arm across my breasts. I lay still, and breathed as shallowly as I could. His head was resting on my hair, tugging at the roots. I pulled it out from under him smoothly. I thought I should wait for a while, but it was already beginning to get light. I could hear the birds waking up. I watched him sleeping. I kissed his mouth. It felt cool and gentle. Sweet dreams, I whispered into his ear. I inched out of the bed, and closed the bedroom door softly.

It took me some while to find the back door key. All the time I listened for any sounds from upstairs. He had drunk a lot last night so I felt safe. On the patio the paving was damp under my bare feet, like the skin on a reptile's back. I had forgotten my robe. Misty air drifted pleasantly over my naked arms as I searched behind some big pots for the trowel. It was starting to rain mistily. There was a strong, unfamiliar, early smell of earth and trees. I kneeled down, and began to dig choppily under the laurel bush. Crumbled mud sprayed onto my nightdress. It started to rain. I could hear heavy drops striking the broad leaves above me.

Eventually I pulled out the red box. The painted surface was already beginning to bubble up. It felt heavy and chilled as I rested it on my knees. I crouched in amongst the laurel leaves, turned the thin, filigree key in the lock, and opened the lid. I took out the plastic bag. With my soiled fingers I fingered the wad of notes through the opaque plastic. I began to sob silently. It felt as if I'd found the door to another world, and it was swinging silently open. I stood up and stepped out of the laurel.

He was waiting for me, his hair sleep-rummaged. You bitch, he said, and grabbed the bag from me. You sly little bitch. He rummaged in the bag. You've been stealing from me, he shouted. I almost laughed it was so untrue. Then I screamed that he was a liar. That I had always paid for everything. I watched as he swung his arm back, and with full force smacked my face. The sound of his palm thumping my ear and cheekbone was not the sound I'd heard in films. I fell heavily on to my knees. I was blinded, as if the blow had knocked both of my eyes out onto the paving slabs. I rested on all fours, my jaw felt as if it was flapping like a snapped hinge. He walked away across the patio, slamming the door behind him. He took all my money with him.

I feel empty sometimes

AFTER I'D BATHED my cuts I put some make-up on. My face in the mirror didn't recognise me. She had different eyes from the eyes I'd always thought I'd had. Her hair was thinner and flatter than mine. She had a disappointed mouth. Then I couldn't get warm, couldn't stay in the house. She lived there, not me. I walked into town. I'd forgotten how long it took. Grit and old wrappers spun around in the wind. People were doing busy things in the main street, going in and out of shops. I wondered what they could find to do. I bumped into Alison. She said she was on her lunch hour, and told me she'd heard a rumour that I'd been sacked. We went into a sandwich shop. She bought me something to eat and drink. I couldn't chew anything.

Alison held both my hands. What's happened to your face? He's done this to you, hasn't he? This is all completely out of hand, she said, her eyes filling with tears. I felt so sorry for her, but I couldn't speak. You don't have to tell me if you don't want to. I can guess anyway. Listen to me, she said. You must come and stay with us. Tom won't mind you staying in the spare room. You know how good he is in a crisis. I told her I had to go home. I could have screamed, there in the café, as I thought about the empty red box upside down on the wet patio slabs. But why, she said, why do have you to? I don't understand you. I should probably go to the police. It looks as if you won't do anything to protect yourself. Why must you go back to him again? I just do, I said. It's hard to explain. I got up from the table. You haven't eaten anything, she said, and started to cry. Please don't, I said. I felt as if I were looking down at her from somewhere shifting and precarious. I know what to do now, I said. Again, what the hell does that mean? she said.

I caught the bus home. As I walked down the garden path I could see the front door was ajar. I pushed through, and walked down the hall. The house had a hollow feeling. Cold air rushed through the rooms. I went into the lounge. All that was left was the TV table and the pee-stained easy chair. A glass vase lay on its belly in the fireplace. Some newspapers lifted and fell with the sound of someone shuffling around in old slippers. I perched on the edge of the chair and looked into the dining room. The table was gone. One chair stood in the middle of the room.

I made an effort to climb the stairs. Only the bed remained in my room. The contents of the chest of drawers and my wardrobe had been dumped in the corner. There was a note stuck to the headboard with chewing gum. It said: *Have run into some aggro. Needed to create cash fast. Furniture all crap anyway. See you.* I got into bed, and pulled the fusty covers over me. I thought I should sleep while I waited.

I dream, baby

I COULD HEAR a snuffly sound. Then I became aware of something warm resting against my side. There was a small, breathing shape under the covers. I was afraid to lift the duvet, but it had to be done. Slowly, slowly I half sat up, and moved the cover down. It was a new-born baby, wrapped snugly in a cotton sheet. Only its face was visible. The baby's mouth was pale, slightly lavender. The colour of a flower kept in the shade too long. I put my face near enough to touch her lips. Her breath was like the breath of a rose that has no scent, just the aroma of itself around it.

I kissed the baby on her lips, letting my mouth rest on hers. I wanted to get inside the sweetness, the unknowing-ness of her as she slept. I did not disturb her. It seemed to me she was already fading, dissolving into the bedclothes. There was a dull light in the room, but around the baby grew a glowy aura. I thought it must be pure love. I knew she wasn't real, but I kissed her again. Her nose was cold. I had to get up to pee so I left her there in the bed. When I got back she was gone. The bed was chilly. There was no nest-like shape where she might have been. No discarded sheet.

There was nothing to do. My house was full of broken, useless stuff. He had taken everything of any worth. I climbed back into bed, and wrapped the duvet round myself. I hoped, before I fell asleep, that I would dream about the baby again. I wanted to see her sweet face. I shut my eyes, and felt my body relax and my head expand until it was big enough for me to crawl inside. I stand up in a room where two people are waiting for me. I'm to look after their child. It's no bigger than a sewing needle. We trust you, they say, and wave goodbye.

Now I walk through crowds of people with the pin-child cupped in my hands. We are in a fairground. Music blows across my face. The baby is uncomfortable. She makes a little mewing sound, so I put her in a blue saucer that has a garland of painted marigolds round the edge. I think she will be safe sitting in the saucer that way. There is a sideshow. Two people are eating fire on sticks, the flames like flickering candyfloss. People jostle the hand that carries the saucer.

Now the baby is floating in a pool of milk. Lie back, my own darling, I say. I hold the saucer up at eye-level. The naked baby is happy. Pink and white. She's smiling with her minus-cule lips, her eyes are dots of light. I know she trusts me. The marigolds enfold her.

Soon everyone has to run. Something bad is moving across the sky. It eats the clouds and stars, sucks in the sun whole, as if it were a tinned peach. An invisible mouth that makes a high frequency sound only dogs can hear. The baby in my saucer is frightened; she is getting sloshed around in her milk, and holds onto the edges of the saucer to brace herself. Her knuckles are white blobs, her cries like a kitten's at the bottom of a deep well. Her eyes flash neon sparks.

Now the thing in the sky makes a deep roaring, like something from before the world began. Like a sound God makes when he's angry. The deep roaring makes the trees explode. Boiling stones spurt jets of scalding liquid. The ground is juddering, is not where you expect it to be, not where you felt it last.

I put the saucer down on the singed grass. I don't care about the baby. The saucer tips a little. The baby's pink body is splayed like a maimed starfish. She is splattered with milk, and quiet now. I run away. All around people are burning, trees are on fire, stars fall with the sound of smashing chandeliers. I run through it all, until I find a cave with a narrow entrance. It smells of mushrooms inside, perhaps snakes, but I fall through dense, writhing leaves and hide.

When there is no more noise outside I remember the baby. My responsibility. My own darling. I think of her shining face, smaller than a shirt button. Her bubbly crown of white hair. Her opaque feet, the mother of pearl nails on her almost boneless toes. How could I have abandoned her? I run out of the cave to search for her. As I run I pull out handfuls of my hair. I bite my lips until they bleed.

Then I find the smashed blue saucer, and sink down beside it. I scrabble in the bruised grass. Nothing. I pick up the broken china, and see fine, white hairs curling, fragments of marigolds. I sob dryly. How could I have been so selfish? So heartless? I sense the parents standing over me. I can feel them smile. They are waiting for me to give them back their beloved baby. I hold up the fragments of china. I have nothing to say. The dream is over. I crawl back to my own room and wake up.

The street outside was quiet. I had that feeling again, beyond lonely, way beyond empty and sad, and I imagined all the sleeping couples wound about each other under their duvets, in their identical bedrooms, up and down the road, up and down the town, duplicated all over the world. I thought of Alison and Tom in their warm bed. Was there anyone else like me? I wondered. Was there anyone so useless, so feckless, they couldn't even look after a dream baby, a non-baby who is actually a sewing needle in a stupid dream?

I lay in my grubby sheets, shiny-eyed, utterly calm. I placed my hands on my belly, and tried to communicate a message to the tiny thing in there. I didn't make any promises. It was early, maybe five o'clock, and I could hear seagulls screaming. They were in their usual frenzy about the worms, fat with moisture, that loop the surface of my lawn.

I innovate with soft furnishings

HE'D TAKEN THE kettle so I boiled some water in a tiny saucepan, and found a tea bag. I picked up the phone to ring Alison, and then changed my mind. I sat on the floor in the empty lounge listening to a fly repeatedly banging into the windowpane. The sound seemed to sum up a lot of things. My tongue was stuck to the roof of my mouth. I couldn't imagine ever talking again. I just sat, all through the morning and the afternoon. As the evening progressed lights in the houses opposite started to come on in sequences that might have been a code for something.

By the time most of the lights had gone out again I was feeling stiff and cold. I made another drink, and held the cup until it got cool. I heard him come in. He was drunk as I guessed he would be. He fell twice as he climbed the stairs, and slurringly swore. I listened to him pee for a long time like a horse, and heard the floorboards creak in my room, then the sound of him falling on the bed. I went on waiting until he had been snoring rhythmically for some time. The last light went out in the house opposite. Eventually the lacey silhouettes of trees became visible on the hill behind the houses. The beautiful, open face of the moon sent its pure beam straight into my head as I sat. I lay down and bathed my whole body in light. I could feel it doing something to me, changing me. Encasing my inch-long baby like a benevolent forcefield.

I climbed the stairs. Each time he snored on an inward breath I set my foot flat on another stair. In the bedroom the faint orange glow from a street light bathed everything. The air was thick and warm. He was lying on his back, his trousers open, both arms resting above his head. I called him three times, each time louder. He didn't stir. His lips were dark red, sucking and blowing. They were the only things moving in the room. I kicked the bed leg, leaned and bounced the bed with my hands. He didn't wake.

I kneeled on the floor beside the bed. My head felt weightless, as if it had been scoured clean by crystals, the inside full of moonbeams. I thought my eyes must glow like lamps from the intense light behind them. I gazed round the room. It felt unfamiliar. I concentrated on the bare wall on the other side of the bed. I allowed my mind to open. On the wall I could see images shaping up. There I was, looking backwards, descending a flight of dirty concrete steps to a dark place. There I was, stuffing ragged, dripping fragments of meat into my mouth. Then I'm slamming my head against a rough wall, then screaming on a huge, swaying bridge, then lying naked and bleeding, surrounded by a crowd. The images whirled across the wall, faster and faster; me blindfolded, me tied up, me crouched on the wet ground, dribbling. And always, me crying. God, how much I cried.

I wiped my eyes on the bed sheet, and stood up. I knew now what my plan was. I pulled the pillow he was half lying on out from under his head. I could see the whites of his eyes glittering in thin crescents. I held the pillow in both my hands, and pushed it down firmly over his mouth and nose. The snoring stopped immediately. I counted up to a hundred slowly, holding the pillow down hard. He didn't struggle, his chest stopped rising and falling. My arms trembled, and my nose was running.

Then I lifted the pillow, and looked at him. Nothing happened. I put my ear next to his mouth, and waited. I could smell his sweat. My hair fell across his face. I reared back as he took a huge gulp of air, and grunted several times. His eyes were slanted sideways. Before he could turn them to look at me I pushed the pillow down onto his face again. This time his legs described slow circles, and he thrashed his arms a little, as if he were trying to run underwater. He was making a horrible noise, a wordless, low bellowing. I had to climb up over his jerking legs, onto the bed and get between them, all the time holding the pillow down as hard as I could. I pressed with my full weight, and still I felt his shoulders rising, but the terrible sounds stopped. I lowered myself until I had my arms crossed on the pillow, and I pushed and pushed until his shoulders sank back and were still.

I sat back, panting. Nothing happened, so I waited, trying to gulp in air silently. I held my hair out of my face, and put my cheek next to his mouth, but I couldn't tell if he was still alive. Then I remembered something I'd seen on a hospital programme, so I leaped off the bed, and ran to the bathroom. In the cabinet I found a safety pin. Then I was standing outside the bedroom. What if he was poised, waiting to jump on me? Somehow I walked back in. There he was, stretched out on the bed. His crotch was wet. I stood by his feet, and undid the safety pin. Then I watched him carefully as I jabbed his instep with the sharp point. I screamed once as I saw his lips move. Nothing else happened, so I stabbed him again. This time his foot recoiled. It seemed to me that his chest rose and fell.

I inched my way up to his head with the pillow clutched in my fists. His hair was dark, and his jaw crooked. I was so exhausted I had become as thin as a piece of paper, my arms useless as straws, but I knew that didn't matter; I had to see through my simple plan. So I pressed the pillow down again, and counted up to five hundred. Five hundred beautiful beats. The first five hundred seconds of my new life. Finally I lifted the pillow, and dropped it on the floor. I kneeled down beside him, and jabbed with the pin all the way from his big toe to his ankle; tiny hard jabs. I told him I was sorry, but I didn't mean it. I kissed his contorted lips. Even then I thought he might grab me, and start everything all over again. But nothing happened. So I left him in the bedroom.

Acknowledgements

MANY THANKS TO my clever editor Ailah Ahmed for her invaluable help, to Jamie Byng and to all the other talented people at Canongate who have looked after me and my book so beautifully.

Likewise to my lovely agent, Cathryn Summerhayes.

Thanks also to my writing group, Edgeworks: Ruth Smith, Liz Porter, Norman Schwenk, Claire Syder and Jane Blank, for being there so helpfully, once a month.

Thanks to the Academi of Wales for the bursary I received to begin this project.

Thanks to Richard Lewis Davies for his advice and support.

Acknowledgements are due to *New Welsh Review*, who published an extract.

Thanks to my children and long-suffering friends who have been so patient while I banged on about my book.

I am grateful to my sister Victoria.

And lastly, for his unstinting support, know-how and all-round wonderfulness, I am indebted to Norman.